Some Species of Outsider-ness

Also by Angela Grey
Spirit Pass: A Jessica Stone Novella #1
Missing and Murdered Indigenous Women &
Girls: A Jessica Stone Novella #2
The Lasting Echo of Lost Souls: A Jessica Stone
Novella #3
Resilience Throughout Recovery
Beyond Quirky
Run Fast, Run Far
Sifting Through a Storied Past
Coteau des Prairies Runaway
Prologue to an Epitaph
A Childhood Lost to the Wind
Secret Whispers
Déjà vu
Of Laughter & Heartbreak
Beating Drum of a Broken Heart
Nostalgic Tendencies, Idyllic Endeavors &
Current Inclinations
Bdote

Also by Angela Grey & Paige Peterson
Lake of Secrets
Dancing Without Music
Echoes of the Past
Echoes at Midnight
Madness and Mayhem
Long Since Buried
Since You've Been Gone

Some Species of Outsider-ness

Angela Grey
Paige Peterson

Some Species of Outsider-ness © 2025
by Angela Grey & Paige Peterson

All rights reserved. No part of this book may be used or reproduced in any form whatsoever without written permission except in the case of brief quotations in critical articles or reviews.

This book is a work of fiction. Names, characters, businesses, organizations, places, events, and incidents either are the product of the authors' imaginations or are used fictitiously. Any resemblance to actual persons, living or dead, events, or locales is entirely coincidental.

Printed in the United States of America.

For more information or to book an event, contact:
<u>angelagrey@ShadyOakPress.com</u>
http://www.ShadyOakPress.com
http://www.angelagrey.com

Cover by GetCovers.com

ISBN – Paperback: 978-1-961841-35-2
First Edition: March 2025

To the love of my life, Robert,
and our four adult children,
Paige, Cody, Chase, & Brooke,
children-in-law
Vince and Angel,
and grandsons Logan and Luke

—AG

outsiderness

out·sid·er (out-sī′dər)
n.
1.
a. One who is excluded from or does not belong to a group, association, or set.
b. One who is isolated or detached from the activities or concerns of his or her own community.
2. A contestant given little chance of winning; a long shot.

outsiderness (ˌaʊtˈsaɪdənəs)
n
the state of being an outsider

—Collins English Dictionary
Complete and Unabridged,
12th Edition 2014
HarperCollins Publishers

Outsideness refers to the sense of self as outside the world of others. It is an early factor influential in developing both the sense of self and the regard for others and otherness. Separation is one form of outsideness, where individuals are separated physically, psychologically, or symbolically from their normal lives.

—https://pubmed.ncbi.nlm.nih.gov/23327003/,
accessed 02.26.25

CONTENTS

Chapter 1

The Art of Disappearing

PIPER

If I could draw myself out of existence, I would have done it by now. Instead, I sit in the back row of AP English, sketching swirling vines around the edge of my notebook, pretending I'm not here, not in this class, not in this town, and definitely not in this skin.

"Piper Quesenberry," Mr. Daniels says, his voice sharp enough to slice through the quiet room. "Would you like to share your thoughts on *The Outsiders* or are you going to doodle your way to a failing grade?"

A few snickers ripple through the class. I don't have to look up to know Savannah Lasky is smirking. Probably already thinking of something clever to post about me later.

"I'm good," I say without looking up.

"She's always good, Mr. Daniels," Savannah says sweetly, but everyone hears the venom underneath. "Good and crazy. A different species."

The word crazy hangs in the air like smoke, thick and choking.

Mr. Daniels clears his throat but says nothing. He never says anything when Savannah talks.

Instead, he moves on. "Alright. Slater Hartmann, thoughts?"

I glance up out of instinct.

Slater Hartmann? I haven't seen him in months, since before the illness. Before, he disappeared from school as if he had never existed. Now he's back, leaning heavily on a cane, his other hand clenched tightly around the edge of his desk as if he's holding on for dear life. His face is thinner than I remember, with shadows under his eyes, as if he hasn't slept in weeks.

For a moment, he doesn't answer. He just stares at the book on his desk, and I can see the muscles in his jaw tighten as if he's fighting an invisible battle.

Then, quietly, he says, "I think… I think sometimes you're an outsider because people make you feel that way. And sometimes, you make yourself one because it's safer."

The room falls dead silent.

The high school AP English classroom feels like a space caught between chaos and quiet. The walls are faded beige, plastered over with bright posters that feature quotes from Shakespeare and Maya Angelou, grammar tips, and the occasional motivational slogan, which peels slightly at the corners. Near the whiteboard, a bookshelf leans under the weight of battered paperbacks: Of Mice and Men, To Kill a Mockingbird, The Catcher in the Rye, their spines cracked and pages yellowing.

The whiteboard itself is smudged with remnants of yesterday's lesson: half-erased vocabulary words and a scribbled reminder about an upcoming essay. In one corner, there's a corkboard crowded with announcements: school play auditions, college flyers, and a few student-made comics pinned haphazardly among them.

Desks are arranged in rows, though some are pushed slightly out of alignment as if neat rows couldn't contain the students' restless energy. Each chair bears the traces of its occupants, like stickers peeling from the plastic backs, scratches on the wood, and initials carved along the edges.

A tall window lets in slants of pale sunlight, glinting off the metal legs of the desks, but outside, the sky is gray and heavy, casting a muted glow across the room. There's a faint smell of old books mixed with the scent of dry-erase markers, and when the door swings open, the hallway's noise spills in shouts, lockers slamming, the sharp squeak of sneakers on linoleum.

At the teacher's desk, there's a clutter of papers: graded essays with red pen corrections, a steaming mug of coffee growing cold, and a laptop open to a slideshow on literary themes. Above the desk, a string of fairy lights zigzags across the wall, adding a soft glow that contrasts with the fluorescent ceiling lights, which flicker slightly, as if unsure whether to stay on.

It's a room that feels lived-in, a little worn around the edges but filled with stories, both the ones on the shelves and the ones waiting to be written.

I blink, surprised at Slater's response because I feel the same.

Savannah snorts. "Whatever."

But I keep staring at Slater because, for a second, it's as if he were talking right to me.

The bell rings before Mr. Daniels can respond.

I gather my belongings quickly, but as I stand up, the room tilts, and I realize I've been spinning inside my head for too long. That happens when I'm close to tipping over when the bipolar highs get too high.

"Piper," Mr. Daniels calls before I can escape.

I pause in the doorway.

"Stay behind for a minute."

Out of the corner of my eye, I see Savannah and Blaine smirk as they pass me by. Blaine makes a swirling motion with his head as he walks past, like the crazy Piper. The usual.

I stare straight ahead, jaw locked, pretending I

don't care.

When the room empties, Mr. Daniels leans against his desk. "You've been distracted lately."

I shrug. "Guess I'm just not that into dead greasers and their cigarette smoke."

He sighs. "You're smart, Piper. Smarter than you give yourself credit for. I know things haven't been easy for you."

Here it comes. The part where they claim to be concerned about you but don't actually do anything to help.

"You're falling behind. I'm giving you a partner for the next project. Maybe it'll help you focus."

Great. The last thing I need is a partner.

"Who?" I ask, already bracing myself.

He glances at his attendance list like this is something he hasn't been planning all period.

"Slater Hartmann."

I blink. "Seriously?"

"He could use a partner, too."

I exhale slowly, feeling the usual itch under my skin. Too much. Too fast. Too close.

"Okay," I say, voice tight. "Whatever."

As I leave, I glance back and catch sight of Slater still sitting at his desk, slowly putting his books into his bag, every movement causing him pain.

I don't know what's worse. Being forced to work with him or feeling like we might have more in common than I ever wanted to admit.

Outside, I pull my hoodie over my head and start toward home. The sky is overcast, heavy with rain that hasn't fallen yet. The kind of sky that feels like it's waiting for something to break.

It's kind of like me.

SLATER

If anyone had asked me six months ago if I thought I'd be back here, I would've laughed. Well, before my body stopped working.

Now I'm back in this same classroom, with the same faded posters on the walls and the same sound of fluorescent lights buzzing like wasps above my head. Only difference? Me.

I'm not the guy I was before. The one who used to skateboard to school, high-five everyone in the hallway, and sit in the front row to crack jokes. Now I'm the crippled ghost who hobbles in on a cane like some kind of tragic movie extra.

Mr. Daniels drones on about The Outsiders, but my leg's burning like it's on fire, and I can't focus on anything except trying not to show how much it hurts to sit upright.

From the corner of my eye, I catch Piper Quesenberry sitting in the back like she owns that whole shadowy corner of the room. Hoodie up. The pencil moves fast over some sketch she's hiding in her notebook. She looks like she doesn't give a damn about anyone or anything, but something about her makes me wonder if she's just hiding.

"Slater Hartmann, thoughts?"

Mr. Daniels' voice slices through my head. Great. My name sounds weird in his mouth as if he's testing it out for the first time as if he's forgotten that I used to sit in this classroom without needing a cane to get there.

Every eye in the room turns to me. Savannah Lasky twirls her blonde hair around her finger, watching me like she can't wait to see me fail. Blaine? He's smirking like he always does. The guy hasn't changed a bit. He's still a jerk, still loving every second of my fall from grace.

I swallow, heart pounding. I hate talking now. I hate people watching me struggle. But the thing about being outside of everything is that you start seeing things other people miss.

"I think…" I start, voice low. I pause, trying to breathe through the sharp ache in my side. "I think sometimes you're an outsider because people make you one. And sometimes, you make yourself one because it's safer."

Silence.

For one breath, I think maybe they didn't hear me.

Then Savannah laughs sharp and fake. "Whatever."

Mr. Daniels opens his mouth, probably about to say something teacher-y and useless, but then the bell saves me. Chairs scrape back, and everyone rushes out as if they can't wait to get away.

I stay sitting, moving slowly because if I stand

too fast, my legs might give out, and I refuse to let them see what happens. As I gather my things, I notice Piper still standing by the door, stiff and tense.

"Stay behind for a minute," Mr. Daniels says to her.

She doesn't argue, but she doesn't look happy about it either.

I wonder what her story is. I've heard the rumors that she's this bipolar, manic, crazy artist girl. But rumors are cheap, and if anyone knows what it's like to be talked about like you're not even human, it's me.

Out in the hallway, Blaine shoulder-checks me as he passes, knocking me off balance. "Watch it, Hartmann. Don't want to break your little stick there," he sneers.

I grip my cane tighter, jaw clenching. I could say something, should say something, but all I can think about is how I used to be him. I used to be strong. Fast. Untouchable. Now I'm just the guy who almost died and came back different.

The hallway of Castle Danger High School

appears to have remained essentially unchanged since the 1990s, with its long, narrow, and dimly lit space illuminated by flickering fluorescent lights that cast a pale glow over the scuffed linoleum floors. The walls are lined with metal lockers, their paint chipped and dented from years of use, some of which hang slightly crooked on their hinges. Hand-painted banners from last year's homecoming still cling stubbornly to the cinder block walls, their colors faded and edges curling.

There's a faint smell of bleach mixed with something older—maybe damp paper or dusty heating vents that haven't been cleaned in decades. Rust-red lockers and dark wood doors to classrooms line the hallway, some plastered with posters for missing cats or upcoming "Safe Nights" organized by the local sheriff's office. A row of trophy cases sits dark and dusty, holding yellowing photos of past championship teams, their smiles frozen in time like ghosts of better days in a town where not much good news comes around anymore.

A few clusters of students linger by their

lockers, talking in low voices, their eyes sharp and watchful, like everyone knows everyone else's business, but no one says it out loud. You can hear the hum of vending machines near the end of the hall and the distant slam of a door echoing from somewhere deeper in the school, just enough to make you wonder who's still here and what they might be up to.

Above all, Castle Danger High feels like a place holding its breath, as if waiting for something to happen or for a secret to finally come out.

As I head to my locker, I catch sight of Piper slipping out of the classroom, her head down, her hoodie still up as if she's trying to disappear. Maybe she will get it. Perhaps she's the only one who might actually know what it feels like to no longer fit into this place.

Chapter 2

Collision Course

PIPER

When I get home, I slam the door harder than necessary, the sharp sound echoing through the open foyer with its high ceiling and polished wood floors that gleam in the soft afternoon light. My bag slips from my shoulder and hits the floor with a satisfying thud, landing on the edge of an expensive-looking, thick, patterned rug.

Straight ahead, the hallway opens into the kitchen, all sleek lines and smooth surfaces, where

Mom stands at the marble-topped island, sifting through a stack of bills as if they were written in some foreign language she can't quite figure out. She doesn't even glance up, her fingers flicking through the envelopes with a tightness in her jaw that makes her look older than she is.

The kitchen itself seems like something out of a magazine, with gleaming stainless-steel appliances, a massive double-door fridge, and custom cabinets in a soft gray that perfectly match the subway tile backsplash. A vase of fresh flowers sits on the island, probably delivered that morning, and glass pendant lights hang overhead, casting a warm glow over everything. On the far side, by the oversized windows, there's a breakfast nook with built-in benches covered in crisp white cushions, the kind you'd be afraid to spill anything on.

Sunlight streams in, catching on the edges of the crystal chandelier above the dining table, scattering tiny rainbows across the pale walls and polished counters. Still, even in all that light and space, the room feels heavy, like the weight of those bills is enough to drag the whole house down.

"Good day?" she asks without looking at me.

I give her a thumbs-up and head straight for my room, not bothering to say anything else.

Inside, I kick the door shut behind me and let out a breath I didn't realize I was holding. My room is exactly the way I left it. It's a mix of organized chaos that probably makes sense to no one but me. String lights snake along the walls, their soft glow already flickering against posters of bands I no longer listen to but can't bring myself to take down. A bookshelf leans slightly to one side, crammed with paperbacks, journals, and random trinkets I've picked up during manic shopping sprees — things like tiny glass animals, candles I've never lit, and a cracked snow globe from some vacation I barely remember.

My desk is a mess of half-finished sketchbooks and pens scattered across its surface, next to a closed laptop adorned with peeling stickers. Clothes spill out of the laundry basket in the corner: some folded, some crumpled in a heap like I couldn't decide if they were clean or dirty. The walls are painted a pale blue-grey, but you can hardly see them under all the taped-up photos and scraps of paper covered in messy handwriting, including lyrics, quotes, and possibly even reminders to myself from different moods.

Without thinking, I throw myself onto the bed, landing among a sea of tangled blankets and pillows, some with bright patterns, others soft and faded from being hugged too much on nights when everything feels like too much. The mattress lets out a soft creak under my weight, but I just sink deeper, staring up at the ceiling, trying to quiet the racing thoughts still buzzing in my head, buzzing with static. Slater Hartmann.

Why him? Why do I have to be paired with the guy who came back from the dead?

I mean, yeah, I guess I got it. We're both school freak shows in our own way. But still—why me? I stare at my ceiling, counting the cracks as if they were stars in a sky I'll never touch. Maybe if I can stay perfectly still, I won't feel like my skin is on too tight. Perhaps if I close my eyes, I won't think about having to sit next to Slater and pretend I'm not coming undone.

SLATER

I make it home slower than usual. Every step from school feels like I'm dragging a bag of cement behind me.

Mom's waiting by the door, her face doing that worried-mom thing she thinks she hides well.

"Hey, honey. How was it?"

"Fine," I say, brushing past her. I hate lying, but I don't want to talk about how Blaine still looks at me like I'm nothing or how standing up in class felt like I was going to collapse.

"Slater?"

I turn around before I can reach the stairs. I said, "I'm fine, Mom."

Her mouth thins into a line, but she doesn't push it.

I head to my room and push the door open, stepping into the one place that feels like mine, even if it's not exactly how I want it yet. The walls are painted a deep charcoal grey, not too dark, but enough to make the white trim and shelves stand out. The shelves themselves are lined with carefully arranged books on architecture, sketchpads stacked neatly, and models of buildings I've pieced together late at night when sleep wouldn't come.

Blueprints, real ones and ones I've drawn myself pinned up everywhere, covering most of the blank space on the walls. Some are crisp and clean; others are smudged with pencil marks and eraser streaks from hours of working and reworking designs. A drafting table sits in the corner, tilted at an angle, with a metal lamp clamped to the side, its long neck stretched out as if it's frozen in mid-thought.

My bed is shoved against the far wall under the window, covering a simple navy rumpled bed, with a stack of pillows piled against the headboard, which is built from rough wood that I made myself.

I drop down onto the mattress, feeling the slight sag in the middle, and sit there, running my hand over the cane resting against my desk. Its smooth, polished surface feels cold and unforgiving under my fingers. I hate that thing. I hate depending on it. But more than that, I hate the way people look at me when they see me, as if I'm already finished as if I'll never be anything more than the kid with the cane, no matter how many buildings I dream up in my head.

And now I'm supposed to work with Piper Quesenberry, the only person in school who might actually be more untouchable than me.

That makes us a team of broken people, I guess.

PIPER

By the time night falls, my brain refuses to let me rest. I pace back and forth in my room, then head to the window like I always do when sleep feels like a foreign concept.

Out of habit, I glance at Slater's house next door, which is a sleek, modern structure with clean lines and expansive windows that reflect the streetlights like polished glass. The place is the kind of upper-middle-class home that looks like it belongs in an architectural magazine, with its perfectly landscaped lawn, symmetrical shrubs, and a front door that probably costs more than my entire bedroom set. The exterior is a blend of stone and dark wood, striking yet cold, like something designed more for appearance than warmth.

My eyes drift upward to Slater's window, a large, rectangular pane set into the house's smooth façade. It glows faintly blue, the soft hue spilling out into the night like the dim pulse of a heartbeat. The curtains are half-drawn, leaving just enough of an opening to catch a glimpse inside.

I freeze when I spot him. He's sitting on the edge of his bed, his shoulders curved inward, his head bowed as if the weight of the world is pressing down on him. The glow from his computer screen bathes him in shifting shades of blue and white, turning his expression into something almost ghostly. His window, so large and open, makes it seem like he's on display, a figure in a painting framed by glass—alone, silent, and caught in a moment of quiet defeat.

For a second, I wonder if he can feel me looking. Then, because I don't know what else to do, I flick my bedroom light on and off once. A signal. I'm not even sure what I'm signaling.

SLATER

My head is in my hands when a weird flicker of light catches my eye. I look up and see Piper's light blinking at me. For a second, I wonder if it was an accident, but then it happens again. I stare at her window, feeling like we're both two satellites stuck in the same orbit, close but never touching.

I don't know what I'm supposed to do, but before I can overthink, I lift my hand and raise it slowly in the faintest of waves. Her light goes dark again. Maybe that's her way of waving back.

PIPER

I sit back on my bed, sinking into the mess of tangled blankets and pillows, my heart thudding way too fast for something that shouldn't matter this much but somehow does. The faint glow of my string lights cast soft shadows across the room, flickering over the sharp angles of my face, making my dark eyes look deeper, more intense like I'm always lost in some thought I can't quite reach. Strands of my long, dark hair fall into my face as I lean back, and I don't bother to push them away.

There's always been something restless in the way I move as if I'm wired too tight for my own skin like I'm a storm always threatening to break. People have called me pretty before, but it's the kind of pretty that makes them pause with sharp cheekbones, full lips that rarely smile, and eyes that see too much. Attractive in a way that's more dangerous than soft, like I'm always one wrong word away from unraveling.

I pull my knees up to my chest, arms wrapped loosely around them, trying to steady the rush in my veins. But beneath it all, there's something else: a flicker of hope I didn't expect, as if maybe, just maybe, I'm not as alone in this town as I thought.

SLATER

I lean against the window frame, my shoulder pressed against the cool glass, staring out at the darkened street below. The faint glow of the city lights filters through, casting soft shadows that trace the sharp lines of my jaw and cheekbones, giving my face a brooding look that people often mention, as if I'm carrying more than I ever say out loud. My dark hair falls slightly over my forehead, a little messy in a way that somehow makes me look even more put together as if I just stepped out of some thoughtful, windswept moment.

The muscles in my arms tense slightly as I brace myself against the frame, lean but strong, though a little thinner than I used to be, which serves as a quiet reminder of everything my body has been through. But there's still something about me that draws people's eyes, even when I try not to let them see too much.

I think about what I said in class today about making yourself an outsider because it feels safer, because if you build the wall yourself, no one else can hurt you. But now, standing here in the blue-gray wash of moonlight, I wonder if Piper's been doing the same thing all along. And if maybe it's time to stop hiding behind that wall — time to let someone see me for real, even the parts I'd rather keep locked away.

PIPER

In the morning, my phone buzzes with a message from an unknown number. Slater Hartmann: "Guess we're partners. Want to meet up to figure out this project?"

I stare at it, thumb hovering over the keyboard.

My chest tightens. Because I don't do partners. I don't let people close. But I also remember that wave from last night.

Maybe we're already closer than I thought.

Chapter 3

Unspoken Things

SLATER

The thing about texting Piper Quesenberry is that she takes forever to answer.

Or maybe she didn't want to answer.

Either way, I'm sitting in the school library, hunched over a worn copy of The Outsiders, flipping through the pages without really reading them. The library isn't huge. It's nothing like the fancy ones you see in movies, but it's big enough for a town like this, with rows of tall shelves that stretch almost to the ceiling, packed with books that appear to have been here forever. Some are bent and faded, their spines cracked from years of being passed from one bored student to another.

The overhead lights cast a soft yellow glow, humming faintly in the quiet, and the dusty smell of old paper lingers in the air. A few mismatched tables and chairs are scattered between the shelves, most of them empty except for me and a couple of kids pretending to study, their heads bowed low over textbooks. The big windows along the far wall let in what little sunlight manages to break through the gray afternoon sky, streaking across the floor in long pale strips that make the dust float like tiny snowflakes.

I sit there, tapping my fingers against the edge of the table, trying to look casual, like I'm just here reading for fun, not waiting around like an idiot and wondering if she's going to ghost me.

Then the door creaks open, its hinges groaning just loud enough to make me glance up, and there she is, standing in the doorway as if she's bracing for a storm. Her hoodie is pulled up over her head, casting a shadow over her face, and wireless earbuds sit snug in her ears as if she's trying to block out the world even as she steps into it. She clutches a sketchbook tightly against her chest, her fingers gripping the edges as if it were the only shield she had, like armor she wasn't ready to lower. For a moment, she lingers there, her eyes flicking around the room, her body coiled tight as if she might turn and leave before anyone has a chance to notice her.

She hesitates when she sees me. Like maybe she regrets coming.

Honestly? Same.

But then she walks over and drops into the chair across from me, tossing her bag on the floor with a sigh.

"Okay," she says, pulling her hoodie tighter. "Let's get this over with."

Charming.

"Nice to see you too," I mutter, adjusting the cane leaning against my chair.

She glances at it, and for a second, her eyes soften as she gets it: what it's like to have something that makes you feel exposed.

"I didn't mean—" she starts but cuts herself off.

I raise a brow. "Didn't mean what? To sound like you already hate my guts?"

She looks down at her sketchbook, fingers tightening around the edge. "I'm not great at this whole people thing, okay?"

"Yeah," I say quietly. "Same."

And just like that, the air between us shifts. It's still sharp but maybe a little less dangerous.

PIPER

Slater's watching me with that steady, unreadable gaze, like he can see straight through every layer I've carefully built to keep people out. Like he sees the cracks underneath, the mess I've worked so hard to hide.

And I hate it.

I hate the way that look makes something tighten painfully in my chest, like he's reaching into places I don't let anyone near. It would be so much easier if he just looked away if he didn't see me at all. Because when no one sees you, you don't have to explain why you're falling apart. You don't have to admit you're anything less than fine.

"So," I say, flipping open my notebook, "the project. What are we doing? A poster? An essay? Skywriting?"

Slater smirks, and for a second, it's unfair, the way he looks good when he smiles as if he doesn't even have to try. There's something about it, crooked and a little guarded that makes him seem like one of those wounded but still-standing heroes from the books teachers make us read, you know, with the kind of bruises you can't see and a stubborn glint in their eyes that says they're not giving up, no matter how much it hurts. His smile isn't perfect, but maybe that's what makes it worse because it feels real like there's a story behind it I'll never quite know.

"I was thinking something easy, like a slideshow," he says, leaning back slightly, wincing as he adjusts his legs. "Unless you're secretly a fan of PowerPoint?"

"I don't do PowerPoint."

"No kidding," he says, eyeing my sketchbook.

I hesitate, my fingers hovering over the edge of the sketchbook, my pulse quickening as if I'm about to step off a ledge. But before I can talk myself out of it, I flip it open to a random page, one filled with swirling, abstract shapes and blurred shadows, nothing too raw, nothing that gives too much away.

Slater leans in just slightly, his eyes skimming over the page, taking in every line and smudge. For a moment, just a flicker, something shifts in his expression. His brows lift, and there's a flash in his eyes that almost looks like surprise? No, impressed. Like he wasn't expecting this from me, and that thought makes my stomach twist in a way I can't quite explain.

"You draw?"

"No," I say automatically, then realize how stupid that sounds. "I mean—yeah, I guess."

"It's good."

The words leave his mouth soft, careful, like he actually means them like it's not just something to say to fill the silence.

I blink, thrown off balance, not sure what to do with the unexpected kindness. I'm used to people brushing off my art like it's nothing, or worse, twisting it into something sharp to use against me. But Slater's voice holds none of that, no judgment, no edge, and for a moment, I don't know how to react to being seen in a way that doesn't hurt.

"Thanks," I mumble, flipping the page like it doesn't matter.

We fall quiet, and for the first time, it doesn't feel awful.

SLATER

I watch her fingers as they move, tapping out a rhythm against the edge of the table, fast and uneven like a song only she knows. There's a restlessness in the way she sits, as if she's holding herself together with threads no one else can see, tied tight and fraying at the edges.

And I get it. More than I'd like to admit, I understand that feeling of barely staying stitched together.

"So," I say, my voice cutting gently through the quiet between us, "what if we do something different? Like a visual essay? You can draw; I'll write."

Her fingers pause mid-tap, hovering just above the surface, and for a second, it feels like maybe, just maybe, I said the right thing.

Her head tilts, and she looks at me like I've suggested jumping off a bridge.

"A visual essay?" she echoes.

"Yeah. Like how being an outsider shapes you. You're an artist. I can write something to match."

She studies me for a long moment, her eyes narrowing slightly as if she's trying to figure out what angle I'm playing, if I'm playing one at all.

"You don't even know me," she says, her voice low, edged in steel.

"Maybe not," I admit, holding her gaze. "But I know what it feels like to be on the outside."

Her jaw tightens, a muscle flickering there like she's holding something back. "You think being sick is the same as being crazy?" The words cut sharp like she's daring me to say the wrong thing.

But I don't flinch.

"I think being different is the same," I say quietly. "And people treat both like garbage."

For a long second, she stares at me, her expression unreadable, a mix of hardness and vulnerability all at once. The tension hangs heavily between us, thick enough to choke on.

Then, finally, she exhales and gives a slow, almost reluctant nod.

"Okay," she says, her voice softer now. "A visual essay."

PIPER

I wasn't expecting him to get it, not really. But somehow, he does. More than anyone I've met in a long time.

As I start sketching, the pencil moves almost on its own, rough lines carving out shapes that only make sense to me at first. I can feel him watching, but it's not the usual kind of watching, not like Savannah's sharp, slicing glances or Blaine's smirking stares, waiting to find something wrong.

No, Slater watches like he's curious, like he's waiting to see who I really am beneath all the walls I've built. And there's no judgment in it, just quiet attention as if he knows what it's like to hide parts of yourself from the world.

And for some weird reason, that makes me want to show him.

"So," I say, my eyes fixed on the sketchbook in front of me, pencil moving in slow, aimless strokes, "what made you say that thing in class yesterday? About making yourself an outsider?"

He exhales, a breath that sounds heavier than it should, and when I glance up, he's not looking at me. He's staring out the window, his eyes distant, as if he's miles away from this room, caught in some memory he hasn't figured out how to shake.

"Because." His voice is quiet, rough around the edges as if every word costs him something to say. When everything about you changes, and you no longer know who you are, it's easier to push everyone away before they walk away on their own.

The weight of that hits me like a punch to the chest, the way he says it, soft but raw as if it's a truth he's lived with too long.

I swallow hard and nod because I don't need to explain that I understand. He already knows.

SLATER

Piper glances at me, and for the first time, her eyes are softer, as if some of the sharpness she always carries has been dulled, at least for now.

"You think people like us will always be on the outside?" she asks, her voice quieter than usual as if she's afraid of the answer but needs to hear it anyway.

I sat with the question for a minute, tapping my pen absently against the edge of the table, the soft clicks filling the space between us.

"Maybe," I say finally because I've never been good at pretending. "But maybe if you find someone else on the outside to be with, it's not so bad."

Her lips twitch like she's fighting a smile, but she isn't sure she remembers how to let it happen.

As I watch her, something in my chest loosens, and for the first time since I returned to this place, this town feels both too small and too big all at once. I think I might not be alone, either.

.

Chapter 4

Almost Brave

PIPER

There are about a million reasons I shouldn't be doing this.

First, I don't hang out. Not with anyone. Not really.

Second, I definitely don't hang out with people like Slater Hartmann, the guy who moves like every step costs him something, like he's fighting a battle no one else can see and refusing to let it win.

Third, and maybe the worst one, getting close to people means letting them see the cracks, all the pieces I work way too hard to keep hidden. And if Slater sees too much, if he sees me, he'll leave because that's what people do.

That's what they always do.

Still, here I am, standing in front of Whispering Hills Casino, my hood pulled up as if it can somehow make me invisible, backup headphones dangling uselessly around my neck like armor I forgot to put on.

The casino looms before me, sleek and modern, with sharp lines and gleaming glass that reflects the night sky like a mirror. Bright LED lights trace the edges of the building, pulsing in soft blues and silver, like the whole place is breathing in its quiet rhythm. The WHISPERING HILLS sign above the entrance glows in crisp white, not a single bulb out of place, casting a cool glow over the polished pavement. Through the floor-to-ceiling windows, I can see flashes of color, bright rows of slot machines, glowing screens, and people moving in and out of the warm, golden light inside.

Even the air feels different here. Cooler, sharper, as if the whole building is too perfect, too put-together as if it's hiding something just beneath the surface.

Slater is already there, leaning against one of the sleek metal pillars near the entrance, his arms crossed as if he belongs here, even though I know he probably feels as out of place as I do. His cane stands next to him, perfectly straight, gleaming slightly under the lights as if it were part of his armor, too.

"Wow," I say as I reach him, forcing my voice to sound casual, even though my heart is trying to claw its way out of my chest. "You actually showed up."

He lifts an eyebrow, a slight smirk tugging at his lips. "You did, too."

Touché.

SLATER

She's different out here, quieter, like the night has taken some of her sharp edges and smoothed them down as if she's trying to fold herself into something smaller, as if shrinking might make her less visible.

I get it.

The world doesn't make space for people like us, so we learn to take up less of it.

"I figured we could, I don't know," I say, shoving my hands deep into my jacket pockets as I glance toward the casino's glowing facade, where sleek neon lights ripple across the glass in waves of blue and white. "Walk around, talk. Pretend we're normal."

Piper snorts, a short, sharp sound that cuts through the quiet, but instead of stinging, it makes me smile more than I probably should.

"Normal's overrated," she mutters, pulling her hood tighter around her face like it's a shield.

"Yeah," I say softly, glancing sideways at her as we start walking, our steps falling into an easy rhythm. "Maybe."

But part of me can't help wondering what it would feel like just to be normal, a regular kid, moving through the world without a second thought. Walking without pain threading through every step, without people glancing sideways when they think I'm not looking, without the hushed whispers that follow me down the hallway like shadows I can't shake.

What would it be like to stand tall without effort, to move without feeling like every part of me is fighting to keep up? To be, without the weight of everyone else's eyes reminding me that I'm different.

PIPER

The casino glows like a world apart, a place that doesn't quite belong to the rest of this town, like its own shimmering planet orbiting just out of reach. Neon lights wrap around the building in ribbons of color, casting sharp reflections on the glass walls, making everything look polished and perfect from the outside.

It's a place where people wear masks, not the kind you can see, but the ones that smile too easily, laugh too loud and hide everything real beneath layers of glitter and silk. Like lies wrapped in sequins, walking on high heels and polished shoes.

We don't go inside. We circle it, keeping to the edges like moths too wary to touch the flame, drawn in but knowing better than to get too close.

I watch as people drift in and out: men in tailored suits that don't quite fit this town's dusty edges, women in dresses that flash under the lights, too expensive to belong to a place like this. They move as if they own the night as if whatever's waiting for them inside is worth all the pretending. And for a moment, I wonder what it's like to step through those glass doors and play along.

"Ever been inside?" Slater asks, his voice low and casual, but I can feel his eyes on me, waiting.

I shrug, stuffing my hands deeper into my jacket pockets. "My mom works there. Supervisor of the housekeeping staff, mostly."

His eyebrows lift like he wasn't expecting that, but he doesn't push, and I'm grateful for it.

"Looks sketchy," he mutters, glancing up at the glowing lights, which flicker and dance as if trying too hard to distract from what really goes on inside.

"Yeah," I say quietly, my gaze drifting to the side of the building, where the back entrance is located, and the workers come and go. A metal door propped open just long enough for the sharp white light inside to spill out like a crack in the casino's polished mask.

And for a split second, I swear I see her again —the girl with the wide, frightened eyes, the one who looked like she wanted to disappear the night I came here alone. She slips through the door like a shadow, gone before I can be sure it was even her.

My stomach twists into a tight, uneasy knot, but I keep my mouth shut, swallowing the words that want to rise.

I blink, trying to focus and ensure what I saw is real, but when my eyes open again, she's gone, as if she was never there at all, like a ghost swallowed up by the glowing lights and shadows of the casino.

SLATER

Piper's eyes are sharp as they track the people moving in and out of the casino, her gaze slicing through them like she's pulling apart layers no one else notices, like she's working on a puzzle only she can see, fitting together pieces that don't quite match.

"What are you looking at?" I ask, keeping my voice low, like if I speak too loudly, she'll slip further away.

She hesitates, her shoulders tense for just a second, then shrugs as if it's nothing, but I know better. It's not nothing, not with her.

"Just people," she says finally, her voice soft but edged. Trying to figure out which ones are genuine.

I huff a quiet laugh, the kind that doesn't quite reach my eyes. "Aren't we all fake in some way?"

At that, she turns to look at me, really look, and for a heartbeat, something flickering in her expression, something raw and unspoken. I think she's about to say something important, something she's been holding back.

But instead, she shoves her hands deeper into the pocket of her hoodie, pulling herself in tighter, as if she can hide from whatever that truth is.

"Guess we are," she mutters, her eyes drifting away again.

Still, I can't shake the feeling that there's something she's not telling me. Something that might explain why she looks at people like she's bracing for them to turn into something else.

PIPER

We keep walking, and for once, the silence between us doesn't feel like a wall, like something thick and impossible to cross. Instead, it feels like a bridge, something fragile but real, stretching out between us with every step we take.

"My dad used to gamble here," I say, my voice barely more than a whisper, the words slipping out before I can pull them back and swallow them down, as I usually do. "Before he died."

The moment hangs in the air, heavier than the night, but Slater doesn't say anything right away. He glances over at me, his eyes steady, as if he knows exactly how hard it is to give that part of yourself away.

"I was in the hospital for five months," he says quietly, his voice rough around the edges. "I didn't think I'd ever walk again."

I stop walking, turning to look at him thoroughly, really seeing him —the way his fingers tighten around the cane, his jaw clenched as if he's still fighting some invisible battle.

"Guess we both know what it's like to lose things," I whisper, my throat tight.

He nods, meeting my eyes, something raw and

honest passing between us at that moment.

"Yeah," he says softly. "We do."

SLATER

For a long minute, we stand there, two broken kids in a town that never carved out a space for people like us, a small city that looks shiny on the surface but has cracks running deep underneath.

She looks smaller now, standing in the glow of the casino lights, like the sharp edges she usually wears, like armor, is starting to crack, slipping just enough to let something vulnerable show through. When she talks about her dad, her shoulders hunch in, as if she's trying to make herself invisible, and for the first time, I realize how much she's been holding in and how much she still is.

And suddenly, I want to know everything about her. Not just the pieces she lets people see but all the stuff she buries: the dark corners, the broken parts.

"Hey," I say gently, bumping my shoulder against hers just enough to let her know I'm here, not running. "You don't have to be tough with me."

She lets out a breath that might be a laugh, or maybe it's something closer to crying, a sound caught somewhere in between.

"Yeah, well," she murmurs, glancing away like she can't quite meet my eyes. "I don't know how to be anything else."

PIPER

We end up on a bench across from the casino, sitting side by side in the cool night air, the bright lights throwing shifting colors across our faces. The neon glows red and blue, pulsing against the dark sky like a heartbeat, but for once, the noise and chaos don't get inside my head.

For once, my brain isn't racing a mile a minute.

For once, I don't feel like I'm about to shatter into pieces.

Slater leans back, his cane resting against his leg, and glances at me from the corner of his eye, dark, thoughtful, like he's turning something over in his mind.

"You're not as scary as people say, you know," he says, a small smile tugging at the edge of his mouth.

I laugh, an actual laugh, sharp and surprised as if it broke loose before I could stop it. "Yeah? Well, you're not as broken as people say."

He grins at that, something brighter flashing in his eyes. "Guess we're both full of surprises."

For a second, we just sit there, and it almost feels easy — like maybe neither of us has to pretend tonight.

SLATER

When we finally stand to leave, there's a shift in the air, small but real. Piper's shoulders aren't pulled so tight anymore, like she's let go of something heavy she's been carrying around too long.

As she turns to face me, the streetlight catches her eyes, and for a moment, they shine, not sharp and guarded like usual, but soft, almost alive, like there's something in her starting to breathe again.

"You want to work on that project tomorrow?" she asks, her voice quieter now, like saying it out loud costs her more than she wants me to know.

But she's asking. She's the one offering and that feels like more than just a question.

"Yeah," I say, holding her gaze so she knows I mean it. "I do."

PIPER

As we part ways and I watch him limp slowly toward his house, his cane tapping softly against the sidewalk, something in my chest feels lighter like a knot I've been carrying forever has loosened just a little and not healed and not fixed. But maybe, almost brave.

Like maybe for the first time in a long while, I don't have to hold everything so tightly to keep it from falling apart. Perhaps there's someone else in this town who gets it, who understands me.

And that thought lingers, warm and fragile, as I turn to head home.

Chapter 5

Something Like Safe

The first thing Piper notices when she steps into the library is that Slater is already there, waiting as he expected her to show, but also as if he knew she might bolt.

And maybe she would've if last night hadn't happened. If he hadn't looked at her like she wasn't some piece of shattered glass that might cut him if he got too close. That thought that look keeps her feet moving, even when every part of her wants to turn and disappear.

Slater watches her as she crosses the room, his eyes following the way she hugs her sketchbook tight to her chest like a shield. But she's not wrapped up in her usual armor: her hoodie is unzipped, and replacement headphones are tucked away in her bag instead of draped around her neck. It's not much, but it's something. It's enough to feel like a quiet kind of victory.

"Hey," she mutters as she slides into the chair next to him, not across from him, as if they're on the same side now.

"Hey," he says back, his voice soft. And when he smiles, small and a little unsure, it feels like they're both figuring this out as they go. Like maybe neither of them must do it alone.

Piper glances at the open laptop on the table, its screen glowing softly in the dim corner of the library. Her eyes slide sideways to Slater, watching him out of the corner of her eye.

"You start the essay part?" she asks, her voice low and almost cautious as if she's afraid of the answer.

He shrugs, leaning back slightly in his chair. "Kinda. I was waiting to see what you'd draw first.

Her brow lifts, skeptical. "You don't want to write around my mess?"

At that, Slater turns to her entirely, meeting her

gaze in a way that makes her stomach twist because he really looks at her, like he sees past all the layers she's used to keep people out.

"I want to write about what's real," he says quietly like it's the simplest thing in the world.

Piper swallows, unsure what to do with that, with someone who isn't trying to twist her into something prettier, easier to handle. She doesn't say anything. She just flips open her sketchbook, her fingers moving quickly over the edges of the pages until she finds a blank one, staring at it as if the answers might be waiting in the empty space.

The silence stretches out between them, but it's neither sharp nor uncomfortable. It's soft, settling over them like an understanding neither of them must put into words.

As Piper starts sketching, her pencil moves in sharp, jagged lines, like she's trying to carve her thoughts straight onto the page. The shapes are rough at first, but slowly, they begin to form into something clearer: two silhouettes standing back-to-back, close but not quite touching, as if they're connected and separate all at once.

Slater watches her hand move, his eyes following every stroke as words gather in his mind, tumbling over each other until they settle into something solid.

"Some people are on the outside because the world shoved them there. Some choose it because the inside feels worse. But sometimes, the outside is where you find those who understand you best.

The words slip out before he realizes he's said them out loud, and when Piper murmurs, "That's good," without even looking up, he blinks, startled.

"You think so?" he asks, watching her more closely now.

She nods, still focused on the sketch taking shape beneath her fingers. Better than I could have said it.

Slater leans in a little, just enough to glance at her page, watching the two shadowy figures become more real with each line.

"You draw like you think in pictures," he says quietly, a small smile tugging at the corners of his lips.

Piper smirks, but there's a softness to it that wasn't there before. "You write like you think in pain," she shoots back, though her voice is lighter than her words, as if it's the closest thing to a compliment she knows how to give.

The words slip out of Piper before she can stop them, sharp and honest, and for a second, she holds her breath, glancing up, bracing for him to pull away. But Slater doesn't flinch. He gives her a small, wry smile, the kind that holds more understanding than most people manage to say out loud.

"Yeah," he says quietly, his voice soft, as if he's not afraid of the truth. "I guess I do."

Piper's pencil slows, her hand hovering above the page, the sketch half-finished and forgotten for the moment.

"Does it still hurt?" she asks, her voice low, as if she's not sure if she should be asking but needs to anyway.

Slater glances down at his legs, flexing his fingers over the cane resting against the chair as if it were an extension of himself, something he couldn't ever put down.

"Every day," he says finally, the words are heavy but steady. "Some days worse than others."

Piper observes him, eyes searching his face, seeing more than he probably wants to show. "Is today bad?" she asks, and something in her voice makes it clear this isn't curiosity. It's not gossip. It's real.

Slater looks over at her, surprised by the question, and even more surprised by the way she asks it, as if she actually cares.

"Not the worst," he answers after a moment, meeting her gaze.

She nods, her pencil moving again, slower now, as she murmurs, "Today's not my worst either."

And for a moment, that feels like enough — like maybe neither of them must face today alone.

Their eyes meet across the table, and for a moment, it's as if something clicks into place as if they both recognize the same storm reflected at them, swirling just beneath the surface.

"I used to think I was the only one," Slater says, his fingers raking through his hair in that restless way people do when they're trying to keep it together.

"Me too," Piper murmurs, her voice soft, as if she's admitting a secret she's never shared out loud.

They sit there in the quiet that follows, not needing to fill the space with words. And maybe, for now, that's enough. It's the kind of silence that feels like understanding instead of distance.

Later, as they gather their things, Piper slides her sketchbook carefully into her bag, her fingers lingering on the worn cover as if she's reluctant to close it. Slater watches her, trying to work up the nerve, his heart thudding a little harder than he wants to admit.

"You wanna hang out again?" he asks, aiming for casual but landing somewhere closer to hopeful.

Piper freezes for half a second, her hand tightening around the strap of her bag.

"Like outside the project?" she asks, her voice low and cautious as if she's not sure if she heard him right or if she's ready to hope for that kind of offer.

Slater shrugs, trying to play it off, though his pulse is loud in his ears. "Yeah. If you want."

She doesn't answer right away. She watches him, her eyes sharp and searching as if she's trying to figure out if he's real and if he means it or if he's just another person waiting to walk away once she lets her guard down.

For a long moment, Slater holds her gaze, steady and patient, not pushing, just there.

Finally, Piper gives a tiny nod, so small it's easy to miss. "Okay," she says, her voice barely above a whisper, but there's something real in it.

Slater's smile grows wider and more genuine this time as if her answer is the best thing that's happened to him all day. "Cool," he says, and there's a lightness in his tone now, like something heavy has been lifted.

As they head toward the door, walking side by side slowly enough for him to keep pace. Piper glances over at him, the edge of a smile tugging at her lips, like she's surprised it's even there.

And for the first time in a long time, this doesn't feel like a mistake.

Maybe, just maybe, it feels like something safe. Something worth staying for.

Chapter 6

Things We Don't Say

Piper isn't used to being nervous, not like this, not the kind that makes her skin itch and her chest feels tight like something is crawling under her ribs. She leans against the porch railing, trying to look casual, but her fingers won't stop fidgeting with the edges of her sketchbook, hugging it tight against her chest like a shield.

She told herself she wouldn't care if Slater didn't show. She told herself it didn't matter.

But now it's five minutes past when he said he'd be there, and she keeps glancing down the road every couple of seconds, her jaw tight, heart beating way too loud in her ears.

Then, finally, she sees him with a cane in his hand, his backpack slung over one shoulder, his head slightly down like he's focusing on every step. And the second he comes into view, something inside her eases, like a knot she didn't realize was there has suddenly loosened.

"Hey," Slater says when he gets close enough, a little breathless, like maybe he rushed to get there.

"Hey," Piper echoes, standing up straighter and brushing her hands down the front of her jeans, trying to act like she hasn't been pacing the porch like a caged animal. This is totally fine.

Slater tilts his head, studying her with those dark eyes that always seem to see too much. "You okay?"

She shrugs, forcing a smirk she doesn't quite feel. "You're late."

His eyes crinkle at the corners, a slight grin tugging at his lips like he knows exactly what she's doing and isn't about to call her on it. "Yeah. Sorry. Nerve pain slowed me down."

And somehow, that makes her chest ache in a

different way, softer, less sharp, because he showed up. And maybe, right now, that's all that really matters.

But the way he says it so casually, like he's used to apologizing for the way his body betrays him, makes something twist in her stomach, a pang she can't quite name.

"It's fine," Piper says quietly, her voice softer than she means it to be. "You're here now."

Their eyes meet, holding for a long second, and there's something in that look, something neither of them has words for, but they both feel it—a silent agreement that neither one of them is going to run.

Eventually, they drift to Piper's backyard, settling on opposite ends of the old wooden swing bench. The wood groans under their weight, creaking softly every time one of them shifts as if the bench itself holds memories of every conversation it has ever heard.

Piper's backyard is the kind of space that feels tucked away from the rest of the world, a little wild and a little forgotten as if no one has tried too hard to tame it. The grass grows unevenly, patches of green and gold weaving together, and weeds curl around the edges of the old wooden fence that leans slightly to one side, weathered gray from years of rain and sun.

A few lawn chairs sit abandoned near the back porch, their paint chipped and peeling, and a rusted wind chime dangles from the eaves, clinking softly every time the breeze picks up. There's an overgrown lilac bush by the fence, its branches heavy with pale purple blooms that spill over like they don't care about boundaries.

The swing bench where Piper and Slater sit is planted under a crooked oak tree, its thick branches stretching wide, casting patchy shadows across the yard. The bench itself is old, its wood faded and splintering at the edges, the metal chains creaking every time they move, but it holds, sturdy in its tired way, as if it has been waiting for someone to sit there again.

From here, the noise of the town feels distant; the casino lights hidden behind the fence, the sounds of cars, and voices muffled by the thick summer air. Out here, it's just them, the quiet hum of insects and the soft rustle of leaves overhead. It feels like a secret place, and for Piper, maybe the only place that feels a little bit like home.

Piper opens her sketchbook, resting it on her knees, but she doesn't start drawing right away. Instead, she glances sideways at Slater, watching him lean back against the worn slats, head tilted to the sky, eyes half-closed like he's soaking in the quiet.

And for a moment, she lets herself watch, wondering how someone can look both guarded and at ease all at once as if he's still bracing for something but hoping it never comes.

"You ever miss who you were before?" Piper blurts out, the words slipping out before she can stop them, sharp and sudden in the quiet, even surprising herself.

Slater's jaw tightens, a flicker of something crossing his face, but he doesn't look away. He sits there for a moment as if weighing the truth.

"Yeah," he says finally, his voice low, rough around the edges. "All the time."

Piper nods, her fingers tracing absent circles on the cover of her sketchbook as if she's drawing something only she can see because she understands it more than she wants to admit.

"I used to think if I could just get it together, be 'normal,' people would stop looking at me like I was broken," she murmurs, her eyes fixed on some spot in the grass like maybe if she stares hard enough, she won't feel so exposed.

Slater glances over at her then, and his eyes are softer, like he's seeing past all the walls she's built.

"You're not broken," he says, gentle but firm, like he means it.

Piper lets out a sharp breath that's half a laugh, flipping a pencil between her fingers, her smile small and bitter. "You don't even know me."

"I'm starting to," Slater says quietly, and when she looks up, she finds him watching her, as if he's not afraid of the mess she carries, as if maybe he has his own.

That makes Piper's chest do that annoying tight thing again, like something's pressing down too hard, and she looks away quickly, pretending to focus on her sketchbook as if the blank page has suddenly become fascinating.

After a long stretch of quiet, she jerks her chin toward the porch, where an old guitar leans against the railing, half in shadow.

"Play anything?" she asks, her voice casual, though her fingers are still tense around her pencil.

Slater blinks, clearly caught off guard by the question.

"You mean, like, music?" he says, as if there's any other answer.

Piper snorts, giving him a crooked smile that tugs at one corner of her mouth. "No, like Monopoly," she deadpans, then shrugs. "Yeah. Music."

He grins at that, shaking his head as if she had already managed to throw him off balance. "I used to. Before…" He gestures loosely toward his legs, the cane resting nearby, and all the things he doesn't say out loud. "I haven't in a while."

"You should," she says, surprising even herself with how much she means it, the words slipping out before she can second-guess them. "Music's like. Another way to scream without making a sound."

Slater looks at her for a long moment, something unreadable in his expression, as if she's just said something far more important than she realizes.

"Alright," he says finally, pushing himself up from the swing with a slight wince, steadying himself. "But only if you draw while I play."

Piper raises a brow, her smirk softening into something almost tangible.

"Deal."

A few minutes later, Slater settles on the porch steps, shifting the guitar on his lap until it feels right, though his fingers move over the strings with a hesitation that says it's been a while. The late afternoon sun filters through the trees, casting soft, dappled light over him, catching in his dark hair and illuminating it at the edges like a faint halo.

Piper watches him from the corner of her eye, sketchbook balanced on her knee as she starts to draw. Her pencil glides over the page, sketching the curve of his shoulders, the way he leans into the guitar, focused, a small crease between his brows as he searches for the right sound.

When he finally starts to play, the notes are rough at first, hesitant, as if they're unsure whether they should be there. But then, as he finds his rhythm, something clicks into place. The music flows out low and warm, soft around the edges, and just a little sad, like a memory turned into sound, something he's carried with him for too long.

Piper's pencil moves faster now, catching the shape of his hands on the strings, the way his whole body seems to relax into the melody, like, for once, he's not fighting himself.

When Slater glances up and catches her watching, she freezes for a heartbeat, but then he smiles, shy, a little crooked, but genuine. And something about that smile makes her chest feel tight in a way that isn't all bad.

"Your turn," Slater says as the last note fades into the warm air, his fingers still resting lightly on the strings.

Piper shakes her head, a quiet laugh slipping out as she tucks a loose strand of hair behind her ear. "I don't play anything."

He tilts his head, a small, knowing smile playing on his lips. "You make art," he says, voice gentle but sure. "Same thing."

For a moment, she hesitated, her fingers tracing the edge of her sketchbook as if she were debating whether to keep it to herself. But then, with a quiet breath, she lifts it, holding it up for him to see, the rough outline of him, caught mid-song, hunched slightly over the guitar, the light and shadows playing across his face. The way she's drawn him makes him look like he belongs to some distant world she can't quite reach but maybe wants to try.

Slater's eyes widen as he takes it in, blinking like he doesn't quite believe what he's seeing.

"Is that me?" he asks, his voice softer now,

touched with something almost fragile.

Piper shrugs, trying to keep her face neutral like his reaction doesn't matter as much as it does. "Yeah," she says, her tone casual, but her grip on the sketchbook tightens just a little, betraying her.

He's quiet for a long moment, his eyes fixed on the page as if no one has ever seen him like this before, as if she's managed to capture something even he's not used to facing. His fingers brush over the edge of the sketchbook carefully, like he's afraid to ruin it.

"It's good," he says at last, his voice rough, like the words are scraping their way out. "I mean. really good."

Piper glances away quickly, her cheeks warming in a way that makes her want to pull her hood over her head and vanish. She hates how easily he can get under her skin, how real his words feel.

"Thanks," she murmurs, her fingers tightening around her pencil as if it were something to hold on to.

For a while, they sit in a comfortable quiet, the kind that feels like a pause rather than an absence, the type that doesn't need filling.

Then, after a long stretch of silence, Piper speaks, her voice low, like if she says it too loud, it'll crack her wide open.

"Sometimes," she begins, her eyes fixed on the ground, "I think I'll never feel okay. Like even when everything's fine, my brain's just waiting to blow it all up."

The confession hangs between them, fragile but real, like a thread she's afraid to pull but can't hold back.

Slater stays quiet for a long moment as if he's turning her words over in his head, weighing them against his own.

"Yeah," he says finally, voice soft and a little raw. "I get that. I feel like my body's gonna give out on me any second. Like I can't trust it to keep me standing, like one wrong move, and it'll all fall apart."

Piper looks over at him, really looks, her chest

tightening in a way she can't explain. And before she can overthink it before she can stop herself, she reaches out, her fingers brushing against his, not quite a full touch, but close enough that it makes her heart stutter in her chest.

"I guess we both don't trust ourselves," she whispers, her voice barely carrying in the stillness between them.

For a second, she thought that'd be it, another truth left hanging. But then Slater shifts, turning his hand until their fingers link together, awkward at first, hesitant like neither of them is sure how to do this. But real.

"Maybe we don't have to do it alone," he says quietly, glancing at her with something soft and open in his eyes, something that makes her want to believe him.

And for the first time in a long while, Piper lets herself hope, lets herself believe, just a little, that maybe he's right.

Chapter 7

Standing Together

School hallways always feel like battlegrounds to Piper. A place where you move fast, keep your head down and hope you can slip through unnoticed, like a ghost no one can touch. The air is thick with the low hum of voices and the slam of lockers, and every glance feels like it could turn sharp in a heartbeat.

But today, as she walks beside Slater, something feels different. For the first time in what feels like forever, she's not walking through the war zone alone.

"Remind me why we're doing this again?" she mutters under her breath, clutching her sketchbook tight to her chest like a shield, her fingers digging into the worn cover.

Slater glances sideways at her, and there's a crooked smile tugging at his lips, not quite a smirk, but close. "Because we're tired of pretending, we don't hear them," he says, his voice low, steady.

Them.

Blaine. Savannah. And the whole polished, poisonous crew that seem to run the school with their perfect hair and sharper tongues, the ones who've made life a nightmare, brick by brick.

Piper swallows hard as they approach her locker, pulse pounding like a drumbeat in her ears.

And, of course, there he is, Blaine Johnson, already leaning against her locker, as if it were his own, arms crossed, with that signature smirk carved into his face. His eyes light up as they get close as if he's been waiting for this moment.

"Look who it is," Blaine sneers, a voice loud enough to draw attention. "Crutches and Crazy."

Piper stiffens, her grip tightens on her sketchbook, but she doesn't stop walking. And for the first time, she feels Slater's quiet presence next to her, like maybe, just maybe, she won't have to fight this battle alone.

Piper's jaw tightens, her teeth grinding together as that familiar heat crawls up her neck, the sharp, burning urge to fire back something that would cut deep and leave Blaine reeling. But before she can open her mouth, Slater beats her to it.

"Wow, Blaine," Slater says, his voice cool and sharp, like a blade wrapped in silk. "Did it take you all morning to come up with that one, or are you getting slower, too?"

Piper blinks, caught off guard by the quiet strength threading through Slater's voice like he's not afraid, not even a little.

Blaine's smirk twitches, his eyes narrowing as he steps closer, his posture shifting just enough to make it clear he's spoiling for a fight. "Careful, Hartmann," he sneers, his voice low and dangerous. "Wouldn't want to knock that stick out from under you. You might fall on your face."

Slater doesn't flinch. His hand tightens slightly on the cane, but when he speaks, his voice remains calm and steady, like steel beneath the surface. "And you'd love that, wouldn't you?"

Piper's heart pounds in her chest, each beat like a war drum, but as she watches Slater stand his ground, a flicker of something else rises like pride.

Without thinking, she steps between them, planting herself firmly in front of Slater, her eyes locked on Blaine like she's daring him to say one more word.

"Leave him alone," she snaps, her voice sharp enough to slice through the air. "Or are you too scared to pick on someone who fights back?"

Blaine scoffs, but a shadow of hesitation now crosses his eyes. "What's the matter, Quesenberry?" he taunts, though there's less bite behind it. Do you need a broken boy to defend you now?

Piper lifts her chin, and her glare is unwavering. "I don't need anyone to defend me," she fires back, her voice steady and strong. "But I'm done letting you talk to me like that."

And in that moment, with Slater at her side and Blaine's smirk faltering, Piper feels something she hasn't felt in a long time: power.

She feels Slater step up beside her, close enough that she can hear the soft tap of his cane against the floor. One hand grips the cane steadily, while the other rests casually against her locker as if it belongs there, just as she does. It's subtle, but the way he stands makes it clear: he's not going anywhere.

"You think just because we're not like you, we're weak," Slater says, his voice low but sharp enough to cut through steel. "But maybe you're the weak one if you have to tear people down to feel strong."

For a split second, Blaine falters, his smirk slipping; a flicker of uncertainty flashes in his eyes. It's quick, but Piper catches it, the crack in the armor.

"Watch yourself," Blaine mutters, but his voice lacks its usual bite as he turns sharply on his heel, stalking down the hallway like he can outrun what just happened.

The moment he's gone, Piper lets out a breath

she hadn't realized she was holding, her shoulders finally easing as the tension drains from her body.

"Well," she says, glancing sideways at Slater with a crooked smirk, her eyes still sharp but lighter than before. "That was almost heroic."

Slater huffs a soft laugh, the corners of his mouth tugging up as if he's fighting a grin, and for once, standing in that hallway doesn't feel like bracing for a fight; it feels like maybe they've already won one.

Slater laughs, a real laugh this time, low and a little surprised, as he rubs the back of his neck. A faint blush creeps up his cheeks, softening the sharp edges he usually wears like armor.

"Yeah, well," he says, glancing at her with a crooked grin, "you were the scary one. I'm just backup."

Piper arches a brow, lips tugging into a smirk. "Guess we make a pretty good team, huh?"

His smile lingers, but it softens, becoming something gentler, something real. For a moment, neither of them speaks, but there's a warmth that settles in the quiet between them, something steady, like belonging, like they've finally found someone who gets it.

"Yeah," Slater says, his voice low and steady. "We do."

Later, at lunch, when Piper and Slater sit together for the first time, it's as if the whole cafeteria tilts for a second. Conversations drop to hushed whispers, and more than a few people glance their way, curiosity and judgment mixing in the stares that follow them.

The high school lunchroom is a chaotic, humming place that's too loud, too bright, and always just a little too crowded. The kind of space where the fluorescent lights overhead buzz faintly, casting a harsh, pale glow over rows of long tables with metal legs that scrape and groan against the tile floor every time someone shifts.

Conversations crash into each other, punctuated by laughter, arguments, whispered gossip, and a constant low roar that never quite fades. Trays clatter onto tabletops, chairs screech backward, and the occasional burst of shouting or laughter cuts sharply through the din, turning heads before disappearing back into the noise.

At one end, the lunch line snakes along a row of glass cases, kids tapping impatient fingers against trays as they shuffle forward, eyeing the limp pizza slices and mystery meat with varying degrees of disgust or boredom. The smell of cafeteria food lingers heavy in the air, a mix of grease, overly sweet desserts, and something vaguely burnt that always seems to be cooking in the back.

Near the windows, the "popular" tables dominate, filled with perfectly put-together students, all with sharp smiles, perfect hair, and eyes that dart around as if they're constantly judging the room. Other groups scattered around the space; the athletes crowded near the center, laughing too loudly; the art kids clustered near the walls, bent over notebooks and sketchpads; loners and misfits tucked into corners like shadows, trying to disappear.

The walls are lined with faded posters for

school events: dances no one wants to admit they're excited for, college prep nights, and anti-bullying campaigns that feel laughably ironic in a room like this.

It's a room that feels like its own world, full of alliances, battles, and quiet wars no one talks about. And every day, when the bell rings for lunch, everyone steps back into it like players in a game they never agreed to play.

From across the room, Savannah shoots a glare sharp enough to cut glass, her perfectly polished nails tapping against her tray like she's itching for a reason to start something. But Blaine keeps his eyes down, and his jaw clenched so tight that the muscle in his cheek twitches as if he's biting back whatever venom he'd usually spit.

Piper picks at her fries, swirling one in a smear of ketchup before breaking it in half, her shoulders tight. "Think he'll leave us alone now?" she mutters, not looking up.

Slater shrugs, but there's a quiet strength in the way he says, "Probably not. But at least now he knows we're not scared of him."

She glances sideways, watching him. She notices the way his hand still trembles slightly when he lifts his drink, like even small things are a battle he's learned to fight without showing too much. The way he holds himself steady, even when it's hard, makes something twist in her chest, not pity, but respect.

"Yeah," she says softly, almost to herself, but loud enough for him to hear. "And that's something."

Their eyes meet for a moment, and in the middle of all the staring and whispering, it feels like a quiet win, like they've carved out a space just big enough for two.

SLATER

As Piper discusses her sketch ideas for their project, her hands move as if they're part of the story, making sharp, quick gestures when she's fired up, her fingers tracing shapes in the air as if she's already drawing them. Slater watches her quietly, taking in the way her eyes flash when she says something sarcastic, how the corners of her mouth twitch up in a smile she tries, and fails, to hide.

It's strange, the way she makes the world feel a little less heavy, a little less sharp around the edges. Strange, and good.

For so long, Slater has felt like he's standing on the outside of everything, watching life move on without him. But sitting here now, listening to Piper ramble about shading and line work, he realizes maybe he's not as alone as he thought.

Maybe there's someone who sees him, all of him, and doesn't flinch. Someone who doesn't look away from the cane or the way his hands sometimes shake.

For the first time since getting sick, since his whole life turned inside out, he feels like he belongs somewhere again.

And maybe, just maybe, they can make space for each other, the girl with storms in her head and the boy whose body betrayed him, finding something solid in the chaos.

PIPER

As Slater leans in, holding his phone between them to show her something, perhaps a song, a sketch reference —she barely registers what. Piper realizes with a jolt that she's not afraid of being seen when she's with him.

She doesn't have to pull on that mask of sharpness, doesn't have to pretend to be tougher, harder, colder than she is.

With him, she can be Piper, with all her mess, her rough edges and cracked pieces, the parts she usually hides from everyone else.

And somehow, sitting there with him so close she can feel the warmth of his shoulder near hers; it feels like enough.

More than she ever thought she'd get.

More than she ever thought she deserved.

Chapter 8

What We're Not Supposed to See

The plan is simple. Just walk around the casino. Do not go inside. Do not get involved. Just watch.

But as Piper stands next to Slater, the sharp glow of the Whispering Hills Casino sign flickering overhead, she knows better. Nothing in her life is ever that simple.

The casino looms against the night sky, sleek and modern, its glass exterior reflecting streaks of pink neon and icy blue that pulse like a heartbeat. Rows of LED lights wrap the building's edges, humming softly in the still air. From a distance, it looks glamorous and polished, like something from a different world. But up close, Piper can see the cracks: the way the back alley smells faintly of stale cigarettes and something sharp and chemical, the faint scuff marks on the steel side doors where delivery trucks have backed in too close.

Slater shifts his weight onto his cane, his gaze cutting sideways at her, sharp and perceptive as if he's searching for all the things she's trying to hide.

"Still think this is a good idea?" he asks, his voice quiet but steady, the question hanging between them.

Piper shrugs, tugging her hoodie tighter around her as the wind slips cold fingers under the fabric. "Nope," she mutters, her mouth twitching into a crooked smile. "But since when do we do good ideas?"

Slater huffs a soft laugh, shaking his head. "Fair point."

The neon light casts shifting colors across their faces, pink, blue, then white, as they fall into step, walking side by side.

They move along the edge of the building, past rows of parked cars and dumpsters shoved up against the back wall, where the bright, polished front of the casino feels far away. As they round the corner, Piper's eyes flick to the employees-only entrance, a heavy metal door tucked in the shadows, half-hidden under a dim security light.

She knows that door. She has seen her mom slip in and out of it a hundred times, head down, carrying bags full of uniforms and exhaustion.

But tonight, standing here with Slater, the door looks different, like a crack in the shiny surface of the casino, a glimpse into something darker.

And even though they said they were just watching, Piper can't shake the feeling that they're already deeper than they are meant to be.

But tonight, something feels off.

The air is thick, heavier than usual, as if the casino itself is holding its breath. The faint pulse of bass-heavy music rumbles from inside, mixing with the distant whir of traffic and the sharp hum of the neon lights overhead. The Whispering Hills Casino sign buzzes softly, throwing shards of pink and blue light that flicker across the asphalt at their feet.

"Look," Slater whispers, his voice low and

tense, as he tilts his head toward the employees-only door tucked in the shadowy side of the building.

Piper's gaze snaps in that direction, and her breath catches.

The door swings open with a soft creak, and a man steps out. He's in his mid-forties, wearing a slick suit that's just a little too shiny as if he's trying too hard to look important. His tie is crooked, and his sharp eyes dart around the alley, scanning the shadows like he's searching for something or someone.

Piper's stomach twists into a tight knot. Mr. Lasky. She knows him and knows how her mom always calls him the "friendly" hotel supervisor, the one who pretends to look out for the staff. But there's nothing friendly about the way he grips the girl's arm as he shoves her through the door behind him.

The girl stumbles, catching herself against the wall. She can't be older than Piper, maybe even younger; her makeup is smudged, with mascara trailing like dark rivers down her cheeks, her eyes wide and glassy with something that makes Piper's chest ache.

"What the hell?" Piper breathes, her voice sharp with shock and anger, as her fingers tighten around her sketchbook as if she could snap it in half.

Slater's hand brushes against her arm, steady and grounding, and when she glances at him, she sees the same wide-eyed tension mirrored in his face.

"You see that too, right?" he whispers, though it's not really a question.

Piper nods slowly, her pulse pounding in her ears, her eyes locked on the girl and on Mr. Lasky's hand, still gripping her as if she were something he owned.

The casino lights flash across the girl's face, and Piper knows, deep down, that they've just seen something they can't unsee.

Piper nods, her heart pounding so hard it feels like it might crack her ribs.

The man, Mr. Lasky, leans in close to the girl,

muttering something too low to hear, his hand clamped around her arm like a vice. When she tries to pull away, he yanks her closer, his fingers digging in deep enough to leave bruises.

Piper's fists curl tight at her sides, nails biting into her palms. The casino lights flash red, then blue, casting sharp shadows across the alley, the glint of his watch, the smear of her ruined mascara, the tremble in her shoulders.

"We should do something," Piper hisses, her voice sharp but barely above a whisper, like the words themselves might shatter the night.

"Like what?" Slater murmurs, his eyes flicking anxiously between her and the scene unfolding before them. His hand tightens on his cane, knuckles white. "If we go over there—"

"I know," she cuts him off, her voice strained, every muscle in her body taut as a wire. "I know. But we can't just walk away."

And then, as if she heard them or maybe sensed them, the girl looked up.

For just a second, her eyes locked onto Piper's.

Wide. Frightened. Pleading.

A look that pierces Piper's chest like a blade.

Her throat goes dry, her breath catching as the girl's terror sinks into her skin, wrapping around her ribs like ice.

The glow of the neon sign flickers across both of their faces, a cold, artificial light that makes everything feel sharper and harsher, and Piper knows, without a doubt, that if they leave now, that girl will disappear into that door, and no one will ever help her.

"We have to get proof," Slater says, his voice steadier now, surer of himself, like something inside him has clicked into place. The sharpness in his eyes cuts through the fog of Piper's panic, and for a moment, she can't help but stare, surprised by the calm in him, by how he's already thinking, already piecing together a way to fight back when all she wants to do is scream.

"You're right," she breathes out, the words shaky as they leave her, her pulse still thundering in her ears. "You're right."

Slater pulls out his phone, his hand trembling just enough to make the screen wobble in the light. "I'll record," he murmurs, a thumb hovering over the button. "Just in case."

Piper's eyes snap back to the scene unfolding across the alley, her breath catching in her throat.

Mr. Lasky glances around one more time, his grip still tight on the girl's arm as he drags her toward a sleek black car idling in the shadows. Its windows are tinted dark, so black they swallow the flickering casino lights, and the engine rumbles low, a sound that makes the hair on Piper's arms stand on end.

The girl hesitates, just for a second, her feet dragging, her body rigid, as if she wants to bolt but doesn't know where to run. But then, Mr. Lasky shoves her forward, rough and final, forcing her into the back seat.

Slater catches it all on camera: the shove, the way she stumbles, the way she looks over her shoulder one last time, as if searching for an escape that isn't there.

The casino lights flash against the wet pavement, coloring everything in sharp streaks of red and blue, and Piper stands frozen beside Slater, her heart pounding so loud she can barely think, knowing they've just captured something they were never supposed to see.

They stay crouched behind the dumpster, the metal cold and rusted, smelling faintly of grease and something sour that lingers in the alley's still air. Piper's hand grips Slater's sleeve tighter than she realizes, her knuckles white, her fingers digging into the fabric as if it's the only thing keeping her grounded.

Slater shifts slightly, leaning just enough into her touch instead of pulling away as he gets it, as if he knows she needs the anchor.

"You okay?" he whispers, his voice barely more than a breath against the night.

Piper swallows hard, her throat dry. "No," she says, the word sharp and small but honest in a way that surprises even her. "But I don't think I've been okay for a long time."

Slater nods, his eyes still fixed on the alley beyond their hiding spot. "Me neither," he murmurs, and there's something in the way he says it, something that makes her chest ache like they're both carrying pieces of the same weight.

For a moment, they just sit there, pressed into the shadows, breathing in the sharp chill of night air, their breaths rising in faint clouds. The casino lights pulse against the wall beside them, flashes of pink neon and blue casting long, flickering shadows, like even the night can't stay still.

It's not safety, not really, but it's something. A quiet moment of truth, like the world has paused just for them.

Later, when they finally pull themselves away from the alley and start walking home, the night feels heavier and thicker. Neither of them speaks at first, their minds spinning in tight, frantic circles. The wind cuts through Piper's hoodie, but she barely notices, her thoughts still tangled up in what they saw.

Slater walks a little slower than usual, his cane

tapping out a rhythm that feels more tired than steady as if everything they've witnessed is pressing down on him.

Piper glances sideways at him, watching the way his shoulders curve forward like he's carrying something too big for one person.

"Hey," she says softly, breaking the silence, her voice careful yet genuine. "You, you were solid back there."

He huffs a quiet laugh, a breath that feels like it's part disbelief, part exhaustion. "You think?"

"Yeah." She bumps her shoulder gently against his, a small nudge that makes a smile tug at the corner of her lips, even though a knot remains in her chest. "Like a messed-up superhero or something."

Slater glances over at her, and for a second, the weight in his eyes eases slightly.

"Guess that makes you my sidekick," he says, his smile faint.

Piper snorts, rolling her eyes but not denying it because maybe, for now, being in this together is the only thing that makes any of it bearable.

Slater smiles, a genuine one this time, small but warm, as if something is cracking open inside him.

"Guess that makes you my sidekick," he teases, glancing over at her with a glimmer of light in his eyes she hasn't seen before.

Piper snorts, grinning for real now, a smile that tugs at her cheeks and feels strange but good. "Excuse me," she shoots back, her voice laced with sarcasm, "if anything, I'm the one saving your butt."

Slater laughs, then. It's a deep, honest laugh that rings out into the night, echoing softly down the empty street. Piper blinks, realizing it's the first time she's heard him really laugh, not the quiet, guarded chuckles he usually gives, but something whole and unfiltered.

She glances at him, taking in the way his shoulders shake slightly with amusement, the way his smile lingers. And for just a second, the weight of everything they saw: the girl, Mr. Lasky, the dark shadows of the casino, all of it fades into the background. It's just them, walking down a dimly lit street, the pools of light from streetlamps breaking up the night like soft islands.

"Whatever this is," Piper says quietly, waving a hand between them, her fingers trembling slightly but steady enough, "I'm… glad I'm not doing it alone."

Slater glances sideways at her, something soft and unguarded in his gaze as if she's said exactly what he's been thinking. "Me too," he murmurs, and there's a quiet weight in those two words that makes her throat tighten.

He hesitates for a moment, then gently bumps her shoulder with his careful yet authentic, as if testing out what it means to lean on someone else.

And for once, Piper lets herself lean back, lets herself feel it, the steady warmth of his presence beside her, the quiet way he holds her up without saying a word.

Maybe they are broken. Maybe the world is darker and sharper than either of them ever wanted to know.

But for the first time in a long while, Piper feels

like she's not standing on that edge alone, as if maybe, if she starts to fall, Slater will be there to catch her.

.

Chapter 9

Who Do You Trust?

Piper's eyes stay locked on Slater's phone, following every jerky movement of the shaky video of the terrified girl being shoved into the car, playing over and over like some awful loop she can't escape.

They sit on the floor of her bedroom, so close their knees almost touch, neither of them daring to sit on the bed like they usually would — as if the gravity of what they've seen has made everything else feel wrong.

The room is swallowed in darkness, lit only by the pale glow of the phone screen. The bluish light flickers across Slater's face, carving sharp shadows along his jaw, deepening the hollows under his eyes until he looks almost hollowed out.

"Should we take it to the cops?" Piper whispers, her voice so soft it's barely there, even though they're the only ones in the room.

Slater's head moves in a slow, deliberate shake. His jaw clenches hard enough, and she can see the muscle working under his skin. "They'll want to know where we got it. Why were we even there? And we don't know anything about that guy, like who he works for or if he's part of something bigger."

"Yeah," she breathes, leaning her head back against the wall with a soft thud. "And what if the cops are in on it?"

The words hang heavy in the air, and the thought sends a sharp twist through her stomach, cold and nauseating.

For a long moment, neither of them says a word. The silence stretches, thick and suffocating like the room itself is holding its breath. The weight of everything they've just seen and everything they don't know how to fix settles heavily between them, pressing down on Piper's chest until it feels hard to breathe.

"I don't know what to do," she finally whispers, the words slipping out in a voice thinner and shakier than she wants, cracking in a way that makes her throat burn.

Slater turns his head to look at her, and for a split second, she catches it, the same fear reflected in his eyes. Not just fear of what they've stumbled into but something deeper. The kind that says I don't want to mess this up. I don't want to let anyone down. I don't want to lose you in this.

"We need help," he says quietly.

The words hit her like a slap, and she flinches before she can stop herself.

"From whom?" she asks, sharper than she means to.

He hesitates, staring down at the floor as if it might hold an answer. "What about Ava?"

Piper's head snaps toward him, eyes narrowing. "Ava Tran?"

"Yeah." He drags a hand through his hair, his fingers tangling in it before he leans forward, his elbows braced on his knees as if he's holding himself together. "She's smart, quiet, and watches everything. And she knows how to dig, like, really dig. She's a tech wizard or something."

Piper's frown deepens as her mind races. "I don't know," she mutters, shaking her head slightly. "What if she thinks we're crazy?"

He observes her, something soft but steady in his eyes as if he's trying to offer her an anchor amid all this chaos. "I think she's already seen enough crazy in this school," he says quietly, the words hanging in the dim space between them. "She might understand more than we think."

Piper swallows hard, throat tight, her heart thudding against her ribs like it wants out.

"And Eli?" Slater adds, more hesitantly now, as if he's testing the ground before he steps forward. "He's well, he knows how to get into places online. If anyone could figure out who that guy's connected to, it's him."

The thought of pulling anyone else into this makes Piper's skin crawl, a prickle of unease running up her arms. Trusting someone with what they've seen feels dangerous, like once the secret is out, they can't take it back.

But when her gaze drifts to Slater, still gripping the phone like it holds something sharp and heavy that's cutting into him, she knows. The weight is too much for just the two of them. They can't carry it alone.

SLATER

He watches her quietly, taking in the way her eyes stay fixed on the floor, her fingers twitching restlessly against her knees as if she's bracing for a fight she can't even name, as if her whole body is coiled tight, ready to snap.

Slater knows that feeling too well.

"Hey," he says softly, leaning in just enough to bump his knee against hers —a gentle nudge that pulls her out of her thoughts for a second. "You don't have to trust them if you're not ready. But I'm not gonna let anything happen to you. I'm in this with you."

Her head jerks up at that, eyes wide and searching his face like she's trying to figure out if he means it if she can really believe it.

"You mean that?" she whispers, her voice thin and fragile, as if no one has ever said those words to her and meant them before.

Slater gives her a crooked, half-smile, something soft but certain in it. "Yeah. I do."

For a long moment, they just stare at each other, something unspoken passing between them, something more profound and heavier than either of them knows how to say yet. But it's there, solid and real, holding them together in the dark.

PIPER

Her heart is pounding so hard it feels like it's lodged in her throat, making it almost impossible to breathe, let alone speak. Words tumble around in her head, none of them right, none of them enough. So, instead, she does the only thing that makes sense: she reaches out and slips her hand into

Slater's.

It's a small, quiet gesture, but when he laces his fingers through hers without hesitation, something inside her eases, like a knot loosening in her chest.

"Okay," she murmurs, her voice now low and steady. "We'll talk to Ava. Maybe Eli, too. But if they screw us over—" she glances at him, eyes sharp, "I'm never trusting anyone again."

Slater grins at that, giving her hand a gentle squeeze. "Deal."

For a moment, neither of them moved, their fingers entwined as if they might hold on tightly enough to keep the darkness from creeping in.

But then, Piper pulls her hand back and pushes herself to her feet in one quick motion, as if she has flipped a switch inside herself.

"Alright," she says, squaring her shoulders. "If we're doing this, we do it right. Tomorrow. After school."

Slater looks up at her from the floor, his smile softer now, but there's a glimmer of something like pride in his eyes as if he's watching her become someone stronger than even she realizes.

"You're kind of scary when you decide things, you know that?" he teases, raising a brow.

She smirks down at him, but there's a flicker of warmth behind it, something vulnerable that she doesn't entirely hide fast enough.

"Yeah, well," she shoots back lightly, "you keep showing up for me like this, and I might start thinking you're not so bad either."

SLATER

As Piper turns away to grab her bag, Slater watches her, something steady and warm rising in his chest, his heart thudding hard, but not from fear this time.

Because even with everything they're about to face, all the danger waiting for them, this moment feels safe.

For the first time since his whole world had fallen apart, with everything he thought he could count on shattered at his feet, he had someone standing beside him. Someone who isn't running away.

And that feeling, that quiet, unshakable sense of not being alone, feels more substantial than anything Blaine or Lasky could ever throw at them.

Stronger than all of it.

PIPER

As they slip out of her room and into the quiet night, walking shoulder to shoulder beneath the weight of everything unsaid, Piper feels the shift deep in her chest. The fight she thought was only hers to carry has grown heavier and sharper.

She's not just fighting for herself anymore.

She's fighting for Slater, for the boy who walks beside her, whose life has tangled with hers in ways she never expected.

And maybe, just maybe, if she can hold her nerve, then she's fighting for her, too. The girl from the casino. The girl whose hollow, frightened eyes refused to let her go.

Chapter 10

The Quiet Between

The night air is sharp, crisp enough to sting Piper's cheeks as she and Slater walk slowly down her quiet street. It's the kind of cold that seeps beneath layers, slipping icy fingers past her hoodie, making her pull it tighter around herself. But she doesn't really mind.

Not with Slater beside her.

Their footsteps echo faintly against the pavement, the only real sound in the stillness. Neither of them speaks at first since there's too much tangled between them, too many unsaid things pressing at the edges. To break the silence would be to break something fragile, something neither of them is ready to lose.

The street is nearly deserted, with houses

standing dark and still, except for the occasional porch light, casting warm, golden halos against the deep, blue-black night. Shadows stretch long across the sidewalks, flickering as a distant car rounds a corner before disappearing again.

When they reach Slater's house, he doesn't head up the steps right away. Instead, he lingers at the bottom, leaning against the porch railing like he's not quite ready to go inside. His gaze settles on Piper, searching, like she's a puzzle he's almost figured out, a secret just barely out of reach.

"You wanna sit for a minute?" Slater asks, nodding toward the steps.

Piper hesitates, her breath curling in the cold air, but then shrugs. She doesn't want to leave yet, either.

"Sure," she says, lowering herself onto the wooden step. The chill seeps through her jeans almost instantly, but she doesn't move.

Slater eases himself down beside her, slower than usual. She catches the slight wince, the way his fingers tighten around his cane as he shifts.

"You okay?" she asks, her voice quieter than usual, the sharp edges softened by something else, concern, maybe.

"Yeah," he says, exhaling as he leans back against the railing. His glance flickers sideways toward her, a small, tired smile tugging at his lips. "Leg is just tired. It'll settle."

She nods, resting her chin on her knees as she pulls them to her chest.

For a while, neither of them spoke. The street stretches out before them, quiet and still, bathed in the soft glow of distant porch lights. A single leaf skitters across the pavement, carried by a whisper of wind. Somewhere down the block, a dog barks once, then falls silent.

And they just sit there, wrapped in the hush of the night, neither one in a hurry to break it.

SLATER

Slater sneaks a glance at Piper when she isn't looking. The way the wind stirs a few strands of her hair, brushing them across her cheek. The way she keeps tugging at her sleeve, pressing the fabric between her teeth as if she's thinking too hard, as if she's trying to chew through something she can't quite say.

He doesn't think he's ever met anyone like her, someone so sharp and fragile at the same time, like a blade made of glass.

"I meant what I said earlier," he murmurs, his voice low enough to almost be lost in the night air.

Piper glances over, brows knitting together. "About what?"

"That you don't have to do this alone. Any of it."

For a moment, she looks at him, her expression unreadable in the dim porch light. Then, something in her eyes shifts and softens. And the sight of it makes his chest ache in a way he doesn't have words for.

"You mean that?" she whispers, and there's the tiniest crack in her voice, a splinter of doubt slipping through. As if she wants to believe him, but doesn't know how.

He holds her gaze and nods. "Yeah. I mean it."

PIPER

Piper doesn't know what to do with the way Slater looks at her, as if she's worth standing beside, as if she's not just some storm destined to leave ruin in her wake.

"You say that like you know I'm not going to break everything I touch," she murmurs, barely more than a whisper.

Slater's smile is soft, a little sad, as if he already knows the weight of what she's saying. "I don't care if you break things," he says. "I just wanna be there to help you pick them up."

Something twists sharp and sudden in Piper's chest, something she doesn't have a name for. No one has ever said anything like that to her. Not her mom. Not anyone.

She swallows hard, staring down at her hands. "I don't know how to let people do that," she admits.

Slater leans in just slightly, resting his elbows on his knees, his voice steady and sure. "Maybe we can figure it out together."

The way he says it is simple and honest, like a promise he has no intention of breaking, which makes her throat tighten.

She exhales shakily, nodding once. "Okay," she whispers. "Maybe we can."

A quiet settles between them, not the heavy kind that begs to be filled, but something lighter, something safer. For once, neither of them must be anything more than exactly who they are.

Piper shifts, leaning slightly into Slater's shoulder, testing and waiting to see if he'll pull away.

He doesn't.

Instead, he shifts closer, the warmth of him steady against the cold night air.

For a long, still moment, they sit there, shoulder to shoulder, gazing up at the sky. The stars fight to cut through the haze, dim and distant but still burning, still holding their place in the dark.

SLATER

He feels her weight against him, just the slightest press of her shoulder against him, and his heart stumbles, pounding so hard it almost aches.

Not just because she's close, though that alone is enough to make his thoughts blur at the edges, but because she's letting herself be close.

She's letting herself trust him.

And maybe, just maybe, that means he's allowed to trust her too.

PIPER

After a while, Piper exhales a breath that's almost a laugh, soft and unexpected.

Slater glances down at her. "What?"

She shakes her head, a small, almost secret smile tugging at the corner of her lips. "Just I don't know. I didn't think I'd ever have something like this."

"Like what?"

She nudges him lightly, the touch brief but warm. "Someone who gets it."

Slater nudges her back, his smile just as soft. "Yeah. Me neither."

For a moment, that's enough. Just sitting there, wrapped in the quiet, the kind of silence that doesn't ask for anything more than what already exists between them.

Then, as the cold finally starts to creep through her hoodie, sinking deep into her bones, Piper pushes herself up, rubbing her arms.

"I should probably head home before my mom starts texting like I've been kidnapped," she says, rolling her eyes, but her voice is lighter than it has been in days.

Slater pushes himself up carefully, gripping his cane to steady himself. "Yeah. You want me to walk you?"

Piper smirks. "You mean hobble me home? Sure."

He laughs, a real, unguarded sound that sends

warmth curling through her chest, though she'd never admit it.

They start down the quiet street, their steps slow but unhurried, side by side. The cold nips at their skin, but it doesn't feel as sharp, not with the easy rhythm of their movements, not with the steady presence beside her.

And for the first time, as she glances at Slater and listens to the soft tap of his cane against the pavement, Piper thinks that maybe, just maybe, she doesn't have to weather her storms alone.

Chapter 11

The Ones Who Watch

The next day at school, Piper and Slater move through the crowded hallway, their shoulders almost brushing, close enough that people are starting to notice.

The air is thick with the hum of voices, the clatter of lockers slamming shut, and the shuffle of sneakers against the tile. But beneath it, Piper feels something sharper: the slow-building weight of eyes on her, the whispering undercurrent that always comes when people think they have something cruel to say.

She doesn't have to turn to know it's coming.

"Looks like the freak show's doubling up," Savannah's voice slices through the noise, smooth as honey, sharp as glass.

Piper doesn't flinch. Not this time.

But beside her, Slater tenses, his grip tightening on his cane, knuckles white.

Savannah leans lazily against her locker, her smirk curling at the edges like a blade waiting to be cut. "Aw, come on, Piper," she purrs. "I get it. No one normal wants you, but crippled charity cases. That's a new low. Even for you."

The hallway feels smaller, the fluorescent lights humming overhead like they're waiting for something to break.

Blaine chuckles beside Savannah, spinning a basketball lazily between his hands, his grin all easy arrogance. "Guess broken toys stick together, huh?"

Slater's jaw tightens, a flicker of something dark passing through his eyes. But before Piper can fire back, he beats her to it.

"Better a broken toy than a plastic one," Slater says smoothly, his voice steady but sharp enough to slice. "At least we don't have to tear people down just to feel big."

Piper's lips twitch, half-smirk, half-surprised

smile. She hadn't expected him to throw the first punch, at least not with words.

Savannah's expression shifts, the fake sweetness slipping for just a second, her perfectly glossed lips pressing together. Then, she recovers, tilting her head, her smile back in place but colder now.

"You're cute when you try to act tough, Slater," she purrs, her eyes glinting with something mean beneath the sugarcoated words.

Piper steps forward, slow and deliberate, her head high and her eyes gleaming with a dangerous kind of calm. The kind that makes people hesitate, even if they don't know why.

"Careful, Savannah," she says, her voice smooth as glass, cool and sharp all at once. "Keep talking like that, and you might show people who you really are."

For just a flicker of a second, Savannah's perfect, practiced smile falters just enough for Piper to see the crack beneath it. Blaine shifts beside her, looking as if he's about to make a smug remark, but for once, he doesn't.

Piper doesn't wait for a comeback.

She turns to Slater and, with the same easy confidence, loops her arm through his. "Come on," she says, her voice carrying through the hallway, loud enough for everyone to hear. "Let's get out of here before their plastic starts to crack."

As they walk away, Piper can feel Savannah's glare, hot and burning against her back, but she doesn't care.

Because for the first time, she's choosing exactly where she stands. And who she stands with.

And Slater? He's grinning as they turn the corner as if they've just won a battle neither of them expected to fight, let alone win.

"You know," he says, glancing down at her, amusement flickering in his eyes. "You're kind of terrifying when you do that."

Piper meets his gaze, her grin slow and sharp. "Yeah. I know."

As soon as they round the corner, leaving Savannah and Blaine behind, Piper exhales a breath she hadn't even realized she was holding. The tension uncoils in her chest, but her pulse is still drumming, a little too fast, a little too loud.

Slater catches the shift, his grin still lingering but softer now. "You really weren't kidding about not backing down, huh?"

Piper smirks, but there's an edge to it, something real, something unsteady. "Yeah, well… guess standing next to you makes me braver."

Slater's smile shifts, something quieter in it now, something that settles deep. However, neither of them says anything else because they have something more significant to attend to now.

Later at lunch, Ava Tran sits alone near the back of the library, half-hidden behind a fortress of books. She's always here, tucked away like she's trying to disappear into the glow of her laptop screen. The light from the tall windows barely reaches this far back, casting the corner into a quiet, shadowy stillness that suits her.

A few tables over, Eli Ramirez is sprawled in his chair, earbuds in, fingers moving lazily over his phone screen. He looks like he's just killing time, but Piper knows better. She knows he's probably halfway into hacking the school's Wi-Fi as if it were his personal playground.

Piper and Slater exchange a glance.

"You sure about this?" Piper whispers.

"No," Slater admits, adjusting his grip on his cane. "But we need them."

Piper sighs, pulling her hoodie tighter around herself like armor, then squares her shoulders. No turning back now.

She steps up to Ava's table first.

"Hey," Piper says, aiming for casual and missing by a mile.

Ava blinks up at them, eyes wide behind her glasses. "Uh, hey?"

She glances between them, suspicion flickering across her face. She's waiting for the punchline because Piper and Slater don't talk to people. Especially not her.

Piper clears her throat, casting a quick glance at Slater with the unspoken, you start, written all over her face.

Slater shifts his weight, fingers tightening around his cane before he exhales and meets Ava's gaze. "We, uh, need your help with something."

Ava blinks, her expression wary. "My help?"

"Yeah." Piper slides into the chair across from her, movements deliberate, as if settling in might make this feel more normal. Slater follows suit, lowering himself carefully into the seat beside her.

"But first," Piper continues, leaning in slightly, "you gotta promise not to freak out."

Ava's brows knit together, but she doesn't brush them off or tell them to leave. Instead, she studies them both, then exhales as she reaches for her laptop, closing it with a quiet click.

For the first time, she gives them her full attention.

"Okay," she says slowly, cautiously. "What's going on?"

SLATER

Slater glances at Piper, a silent question in his eyes:

How much do we say?

Piper hesitates, the weight of it pressing against her ribs, then exhales and meets Ava's gaze head-on.

"We saw something," she says, her voice lower now, steady but edged with something sharp. "At the casino. Something bad."

Ava's eyes widen slightly, but she doesn't jump in with questions. She just watches them, waiting.

Slater pulls out his phone, unlocking it with a quick swipe before sliding it across the table.

"Just watch," he says, his voice quieter than before.

Ava hesitates, fingers hovering over the screen, but then she taps play. The grainy video flickers to life, and as soon as she sees him, Mr. Lasky, shoving a terrified girl into the backseat of a car, all the color drains from her face.

Her breath hitches. "Oh my god."

Piper studies her, searching for doubt, waiting for Ava to dismiss it, to say it's nothing, that they're overreacting.

But Ava looks up, and when her eyes meet Piper's, there's no hesitation. No doubt. Just something steady, something sharp with understanding.

"I believe you," she says.

Relief crashes through Piper so fast it nearly knocks the breath from her lungs and makes her dizzy.

"Okay," Slater says, his voice quiet but firm. "So… can you help us figure out what to do? Who to trust? We don't want to go to the wrong people."

Ava takes a slow, measured breath as if she's turning the question over in her mind before nodding. "Yeah. I can do that. But…" She hesitates, then glances toward the other side of the library. "I think Eli should help too."

Piper stiffens instinctively. "Ramirez?"

Ava nods, leaning in slightly. "He's good at finding things. Online. If this guy's part of something bigger… Eli could help us track it down."

Piper presses her lips together, casting a

sideways glance at Slater. She doesn't like bringing in more people and trusting someone she barely knows.

"You trust him?" she asks, voice careful.

Ava shrugs, but there's certainty in the way she says, "More than I trust anyone else."

PIPER

Piper doesn't like it. She doesn't like letting more people in, especially not on something this dangerous, this raw. It feels too exposed, too uncertain, like handing over something fragile and hoping no one drops it.

But then she looks at Ava again. Piper sees the way Ava watched that video without turning away, the way she didn't hesitate to believe them.

They need help.

Piper exhales, forcing down the instinct to shut this down, to keep it just between her and Slater.

"Alright," she says, her voice tight but steady. "Let's get him."

Ava doesn't waste a second. She lifts a hand and waves Eli over.

Across the library, Eli Ramirez pulls out an earbud, his gaze flicking toward them as he pushes back his chair. He strolls over, exuding lazy confidence, dropping into the seat as if he belongs there, his usual smirk already in place.

"What's up, Tran?" he says, cocking an eyebrow as he looks between them. "Didn't think you ran with the Quesenberry-Hartmann crew."

Ava shoots him a look, one that shuts down whatever joke he is about to make. "This is serious, Eli."

The smirk lingers for half a second before fading slightly. He studies her expression, then leans forward. "Okay?"

Without a word, Slater slides the phone across the table.

Eli picks it up, pressing play, his posture shifting as he watches. At first, his expression is unreadable, but then his smirk disappears completely, his brows knitting together. He leans in, his eyes narrowing as the grainy footage plays out: the shove, the terrified girl, the car door slamming shut.

When the video ends, he exhales slowly, letting out a low whistle.

"That's Lasky," he mutters, his voice lower now, like he's suddenly aware of the space around them. "The hotel guy." He glances around, scanning the library like someone might be listening. Then, quieter, more uncertain than Piper's ever heard him as he asks, "What the hell is he doing?"

Piper arches a brow, arms crossed. "We were hoping you could help figure that out."

Eli leans back slightly, eyes flicking between them, weighing his options. "And if I say no?"

Piper doesn't hesitate. "Then we do it ourselves," she says, her voice cold, steady. "But this girl, whoever she is, she's running out of time."

Silence stretches between them, thick with unspoken tension. Eli holds her gaze, his usual smirk nowhere in sight. Then, after a beat, he exhales sharply and nods.

"Alright," he mutters, rolling his shoulders.

"I'm in. Let me see what I can dig up."

Ava released a slow breath as if she hadn't realized she'd been holding it.

Piper doesn't say anything, but she feels it, the shift.

The beginning of something. A team.

Shaky. Uncertain. But real.

SLATER

Slater watches Piper watching them: Ava and Eli, bent over the screen, already deep in discussion. And for the first time since this whole thing started, it doesn't feel like it's just him and Piper against the world.

The weight of it isn't on their shoulders alone anymore.

Slater leans in slightly, his voice low but certain. "We'll figure this out. Together."

Piper turns to him, something shifting in her expression. Something quieter, less guarded.

And when she finally speaks, her voice isn't edged in doubt or hesitation.

"Yeah," she says, and this time, it sounds like she means it.

Chapter 12

The Things We Shouldn't Know

It doesn't take long for Eli to work his magic.

By the next day, they're all crammed into a quiet corner of the library, a space no one pays attention to, dimly lit and tucked behind tall shelves stacked with books that smell of dust and old paper. They sit close, heads bent together, their voices low so no one can overhear.

Eli's laptop is open, the screen casting a faint glow across his face. His fingers move fast. Fluid, like breaking into places he shouldn't, is as natural as breathing.

"Alright," he mutters, eyes fixed on the screen. "So, our friend Lasky? Not just a hotel manager."

Piper leans in pulse quickening. "What do you mean?"

Eli finally looks up, his usual smirk nowhere to be found. "I mean, he's got connections. Real ones. Hidden bank accounts under shell companies, you know, offshore stuff. And there's money moving through those accounts that don't add up for a guy whose biggest headache should be room service complaints."

Ava stiffens beside him, and Piper feels her stomach drop.

This isn't just a bad guy doing bad things.

This is bigger.

"How much money?" Slater asks quietly, his grip tightening on his cane.

Eli exhales, low and measured. "Hundreds of thousands, probably more."

Ava bites her lip as her fingers scroll quickly over her tablet screen. Her brows knit together as she reads, her expression darkening. "And get this: there are records of girls checking into the hotel under fake names—many of them. No ID, no credit card trails. Sometimes, they stay a night. Sometimes just a few hours."

Piper's stomach twists, a cold weight settling deep in her gut.

She looks at Ava, forcing the words out even as her throat tightens. "Are you saying what I think you're saying?" Her voice is sharper than she means it to be, but she doesn't care.

Ava lifts her gaze, her face grim, unflinching.

"Yeah," she says. "I think this is a trafficking ring. And Lasky's either running it… or working for someone who is."

SLATER

The words hit Slater like a punch to the gut.

He knew something was wrong. They both did. But this? This is darker than anything he was prepared for.

His stomach turns, a slow, sinking weight settling in his chest. He glances at Piper and sees the tension in her jaw, the way her hands have curled into fists in her lap, white-knuckled and unmoving.

He wants to say something, anything, to make

it better. But there's nothing. No words that could make this less real, less horrifying.

After a long, heavy moment, Piper finally speaks, her voice rough, scraped raw. "Who are the girls?"

Eli exhales sharply, shaking his head. "Can't figure that out yet. But I'm trying to trace the fake names to real IDs."

Slater swallows hard. His throat feels tight, his fingers gripping his knee like he needs to ground himself.

"How many?" he forces out, dreading the answer.

Eli hesitates, his fingers tapping against the edge of his laptop. Then, quietly, too quietly, he says, "More than a dozen. Probably more we don't know about."

PIPER

Piper feels like the walls are closing in like the air in the library is suddenly too thin.

Her mind flashes through all those faces. The missing girl posters are pinned to bulletin boards at gas stations and outside grocery stores and tacked to streetlights, where the paper curls at the edges from wind and rain. Girls who vanished without a trace, their smiles frozen in time, their names slowly fading from people's minds.

She remembers the girl at the casino. The one with panic in her eyes, the one who looked at her as if she were the last hope she had.

A sharp, burning pressure builds in her chest. Then, suddenly, snap.

"Why isn't anyone doing anything?" Piper bursts out, her voice sharp enough to cut. She pushes back from the table, pacing the narrow space between the bookshelves, hands shaking. "If this is happening right under everyone's noses, then why aren't the cops stopping it?"

Ava looks up, fingers curled around the edge of her tablet, her expression serious, unwavering. "Because people like Lasky know how to hide. And if anyone's protecting him—"

"—they're helping him keep it going," Slater finishes, his voice quieter, heavier.

Piper stops mid-step, her hand shaking as she drags it through her hair. The weight of it all presses down on her, an unbearable, suffocating thing. "So what?" she demands, turning back to them. "We're supposed to do nothing. Just sit here, watch this happen, and hope someone else figures it out?"

Eli shakes his head, shutting his laptop with a sharp click. His usual smirk is gone, replaced with something far more serious.

"No way," he says, leaning forward. "We're not walking away. But if we're gonna take them down, we have to be smart about it."

SLATER

Slater leans forward, resting his elbows on his knees, his brow furrowed in thought. The library feels quieter now, the air is heavy with the weight of what they're about to do.

"We need proof," he says finally, his voice low,

deliberate. "Not just of the girl we saw but of all of it. Connections. Money trails. Names."

Ava nods, already pulling up something on her tablet. "We'll get it," she says, her tone steady. "But we need to be careful. If Lasky finds out we're looking into him—"

"He won't," Piper cuts in, her voice firm. Too firm. She needs to believe that. "We'll be careful."

Her pulse is still hammering in her chest, and deep down, she knows the truth. She knows there's no way to stay entirely safe when you're going up against people like this.

They're stepping into something dangerous.

And there's no turning back now.

PIPER

Piper glances at Slater, her chest still tight, the weight of everything pressing down on her. But when he meets her gaze, there's something steady in his eyes, something sure, unshaken. It anchors her, pulling her back from the edge, making her feel just a little less like she's drowning.

"We can do this," he says softly, his voice meant just for her. A quiet promise.

She swallows hard, nodding. "Yeah." Her voice isn't as steady as his, but there's resolve in it.

We must.

ELI

Eli's fingers fly across the keyboard, the glow of his laptop screen reflecting in his eyes. Lines of data scroll past, numbers and names shifting as he pulls up more records, piecing together a puzzle no one else seems willing to see.

"We'll start with the fake names," he murmurs, half to himself, half to them. "Follow the money. And maybe, if we're lucky, find out who's really pulling the strings behind Lasky."

Ava watches him, her fingers curled around the edge of the table. Her voice is quieter when she asks, "And then?"

Eli pauses, looking up. His usual easygoing

smirk is gone, replaced by something colder and sharper.

"Then we take them down," he says, his voice low but certain.

PIPER

Piper sinks back into her chair, her legs unsteady beneath her. It feels like the floor isn't quite solid anymore, like the weight of what they've just decided is pressing down on her, making it hard to breathe.

Her hands curl into fists against her lap, trying to stop the faint tremor in her fingers. Her pulse pounds in her ears, a steady, insistent drumbeat.

Because now it's real. Not just suspicion. Not just a theory. Now, they're in it. And there's no turning back.

SLATER

As Slater watches Piper, her eyes sharp, burning with determination, he feels an odd mix of fear and pride settle in his chest.

They're in way over their heads.

But they're in it together.

As they step out of the library, Piper lingers for a moment, glancing over her shoulder. Ava and Eli are already hunched over their screens, fingers flying, poring through files like they've done this a thousand times. The glow of the laptop screens reflects off Ava's glasses, Eli muttering something under his breath as he pulls up another record.

"They're good," Slater murmurs beside her.

"Yeah," Piper agrees, but there's something distant in her voice, something thoughtful.

Then she looks up at him, and for a second, the fire in her eyes dims, replaced with something raw. Something real.

"But you're the only one I trust to have my back," she admits, her voice quieter now, as if the words are fragile as if saying them out loud might make them too real.

Slater's breath catches, his fingers tightening slightly around his cane.

But then he smiles—soft, steady, "Always.".

Chapter 13

Too Close to the Fire

Eli paces the length of the library's secluded corner, his laptop tucked under one arm as if he's carrying live explosives. His usual smirk is nowhere to be seen, replaced by something sharp and serious, his eyes flickering with barely contained energy.

"You guys better sit down for this," he says, his gaze sweeping over Piper, Slater, and Ava.

They're back in their usual spot, but the air feels different now as if it's thicker and heavier. Like they've crossed some invisible line, stepped too far into the dark, and there's no way to turn back.

Piper doesn't move. She narrows her eyes, arms crossed. "Just say it, Eli."

Eli takes a breath, then lets it out, raking a hand through his hair. "So, I was digging into Lasky's accounts. Following where the money was coming from, right?" He shifts his weight, glancing at each of them before continuing. "And guess who's been sending him regular transfers, huge ones?"

Slater stiffens beside Piper, and his grip on his cane tightens. "Who?" he asks, but there's something in his voice tightness as if he already knows the answer won't be good.

Eli glances around, lowering his voice even though there's no one near enough to hear.

"Savannah's dad."

The words hit like a punch to the ribs, knocking the air from Piper's lungs.

Her mouth drops open. "Wait. What?"

"Yeah." Eli nods grimly, his expression dark. It turns out her dad isn't just running the hotel. He's funding this whole thing. The fake accounts, the money moving through Lasky. It all traces back to him."

Slater exhales sharply, dragging his hand down his face like he's trying to wipe away the weight of what they've just learned. "So, Savannah's been tormenting you for years, and her dad's running a trafficking ring right under everyone's nose."

Piper lets out a short, bitter laugh, but there's no humor in it. Just disbelief. Just something sharp-edged and unraveling. "Of course," she mutters, voice tight with something that feels dangerously close to panic. "Because this town's just one big mess of secrets, right?"

She starts pacing, fast and erratic, her boots scuffing against the floor. Her hands tangle in her hair, fingers pulling at the strands as if she's trying to yank her thoughts into place physically. If she tugs hard enough, everything will fall into place.

"Piper," Slater says carefully, watching her like she might break apart right in front of him. His voice is steady and grounding. "Hey. It's okay."

"It's not okay," Piper snaps, spinning around so fast that her hoodie twists at the collar. Her eyes burn, wild with panic, her breath sharp and uneven. "This is bigger than we thought. Way bigger. Savannah's dad? You know what that means? No one's gonna help us! They run this town!"

Slater takes a step towards her. "Piper?"

"I can't—" The words cut off as she sucks in a breath, too fast, too shallow. The room tilts, the walls pressing in, her heartbeat a frantic, pounding rhythm in her ears. Her hands shake at her sides, her fingers twitching as if they don't know what to do, as if she needs to move, needs to run.

Slater reaches out, his touch light but firm as his fingers close gently around her wrist.

"Hey, hey, breathe. Just breathe, okay?" His voice is steady and calm, an anchor against the storm raging in her head.

Piper swallows hard, trying to force air into her lungs and slow the frantic buzzing in her skull. But everything is too much. The colors in the room are too bright, the edges of the bookshelves too sharp, her thoughts too fast, too tangled, crashing over each other like waves in a storm.

Her skin prickles, her whole body thrumming like it might shatter apart at any second.

Ava steps in carefully, her voice gentle but certain. "Piper, we're going to figure this out.

Together. You're not alone in this."

But Piper shakes her head, stepping back just slightly like she's trying to put distance between herself and the impossible weight of all of this. Her breath is still coming fast, her pulse hammering beneath her skin.

"You don't get it," she says, voice tight, nearly breaking. "If Savannah's dad is involved, we're screwed. Like really screwed. He has money, power."

"Which is why we're going to be smart about this," Eli cuts in, his voice quieter than usual, softer than Piper expected.

She looks at him, startled by the absence of sarcasm and bravado.

"We don't make a move until we know exactly what we're up against," he says, his dark eyes steady, serious. "We do this the right way."

As they talk, Ava's gaze flickers toward the library door, and suddenly, she goes still. Her eyes widen just slightly, but it's enough.

Piper catches it instantly. "What?" she asks

sharply, twisting around to follow Ava's line of sight.

But Ava shakes her head too quickly, her voice coming out in a rush. "Nothing." Lie.

Piper knows it the second she hears it. And the way Ava's fingers tighten around her tablet, the way she casts another furtive glance over her shoulder as if she can't help herself, only confirms it.

Slater notices, too.

Later, when they're walking out together, Slater leans in, his voice low. "Ava saw something. Or someone."

Piper nods tightly, her pulse still thrumming under her skin. She already knows.

And she has a horrible feeling she knows who.

Once they step outside, the cool air does nothing to steady Piper's pulse. She starts pacing again, her boots scuffing against the pavement, her mind spinning too fast, too loud.

"They're gonna come for us, Slater," she says, voice sharp with panic. "If they know what we know."

"Stop."

Slater steps in front of her, cutting off her path, his expression unwavering. His presence is solid and grounding.

"Look at me," he says firmly.

She does, her breath coming fast, her chest rising and falling like she can't get enough air. Her eyes are wide and frantic.

"We're not running," Slater says, his voice steady, an anchor against the storm raging inside her. "You're not alone in this. I've got you, okay?"

Her breath shudders out, but she doesn't look away.

"I've got you," he says again, softer now as a quiet promise meant just for her.

Piper swallows hard. "Okay," she whispers, though she's not sure she believes it yet.

Still, when Slater reaches for her hand, she doesn't pull away. She lets him take it.

They sit together on the low stone wall outside the school, the rough edge cool beneath their hands, the scent of asphalt and faint traces of autumn in the air. The parking lot is nearly empty now, the last few students trickling away, their voices fading into the evening hush.

Piper leans her head against Slater's shoulder, exhaling slowly as the quiet wraps around them like a fragile shield against everything waiting beyond it.

"I'm scared," she murmurs, the words barely more than a breath.

Slater shifts just slightly, just enough to press a little closer, a steady warmth against her side. "Me too," he admits. "But we'll figure it out. You and me. Ava and Eli."

She nods, her eyes half-shut, exhaustion threading through her limbs. The weight in her chest doesn't vanish, but it eases slightly.

For now, that's enough.

Because even though the world feels like it's pressing in, ready to swallow them whole.

She's not alone anymore.

And neither is he.

Chapter 14

The Line We Cross

The next day, Piper feels it. Something is off.

It's not the usual chaos in her head, not the way she sometimes spins out, caught in a spiral of her own thoughts. This is different.

This is the world shifting, the air pressing too thick around her like the ground is getting ready to crack open beneath her feet.

She sits on the front steps of the school next to Slater, her sketchbook balanced on her knees. She tries to draw, to lose herself in the movement of the pencil, but her hands won't stop shaking. The lines come out too fast, too sharp, and jagged where they should be smooth.

Slater watches her, that quiet, careful look

settling in his eyes, the one he gets when he knows she's not okay but isn't going to push.

"You good?" he asks, his voice even, steady.

"Yeah," she says automatically, too fast, too light.

Slater doesn't call her out. He doesn't need to. Instead, he rests a hand gently on her knee, a quiet, wordless anchor.

Piper exhales shakily, pressing her palm over his hand. The world still feels unsteady beneath her, but at least she has something to hold on to.

"Hey, I almost forgot," Eli's voice slices through the quiet, his footsteps quick as he jogs up, phone in hand. His usual smirk is nowhere to be seen. There's something off in the way he moves, in the way his eyes flick around before locking onto them. "You guys need to see this," he says.

Piper's stomach knots. The look on his face is enough to send ice down her spine.

Eli holds out his phone, and the moment she sees the screen, her breath stutters.

It's a picture. Of them. Blurry but

unmistakable. Of Piper and Slater, sitting right here on the school steps. Taken from a distance.

And underneath, the message is worse. Some people need to learn when to stop digging.

Piper's heart slams against her ribs, a rush of cold panic flooding her veins.

"Who sent that?" Slater asks, his voice low, razor-sharp.

Eli glances around, lowering his voice even more. "Blocked number," he mutters. "But if I had to guess?" His jaw tightens. "Lasky. Or someone working for him."

Piper shoots to her feet too fast, her vision tilting as panic crashes through her. She starts pacing, her boots scuffing against the pavement, her hands tangling in her hair as if she can physically hold herself together.

"I knew it," she breathes, voice tight, cracking at the edges. "I knew we shouldn't have done this. He knows. He knows, and now we're next."

Slater stands slowly, steady as she unravels, reaching for her. "Piper?"

"No, Slater!" Her voice breaks, louder than she intended, echoing into the open space. "You don't get it! I can't—"

Her breath is coming too fast now, the world spinning at the edges, her thoughts unraveling faster than she can catch them. Her pulse thrums in her ears, drowning out everything else.

"Hey."

Slater's voice is quiet but firm, and suddenly, he's there, stepping in close, his hands grounding as they settle gently on her shoulders. His touch is warm and steady, not holding her down, just holding her here.

"Look at me," he says.

She does, barely. Her eyes wide, wild, fear flickering behind them like a storm barely contained.

"You're not alone," Slater reminds her, his voice a tether pulling her back. "Remember? We do this together." He squeezes her shoulders lightly. "Breathe, Piper. Just breathe."

She sucks in a breath, shaky and uneven, trying

to match the steadiness in his voice.

"Good," he murmurs, softer now. "Again."

And this time, she does.

Slowly, the panic loosens its claws, retreating inch by inch, though it leaves behind a restless hum beneath her skin. Her hands are still trembling, her pulse still too fast, her body coiled tight with leftover adrenaline. Fear lingers at the edges, not gone, but no longer drowning her.

Ava arrives next, her sharp eyes scanning the scene, widening slightly when she sees Piper, who is pale, still trembling, her breath not quite even. But she doesn't say anything. She just sits down close, a quiet, steady presence, offering warmth without words.

Piper exhales slowly, the last remnants of panic fading to something steadier, something she can hold onto.

Then Eli breaks the silence, "If they're already watching us," he says carefully, his voice low, measured, "then we have to move faster. We need proof. Something that ties this directly to

Savannah's dad. Something so real they can't bury it."

"Like what?" Slater asks, his hand still rubbing slow circles on Piper's back, grounding her.

"Paperwork. Photos. Security footage, whatever's in that hotel." Eli's eyes flicker with something sharp, calculating.

Ava nods, pushing her glasses up as she leans forward. "And I know where they keep the files. There's a back office. My mom used to clean there. She told me once that high rollers get tracked for 'special services.'" Her voice tightens slightly. "I bet if this goes as deep as we think, that's where the evidence is."

A moment of silence warms over them.

Then Piper lifts her head, her voice steady now, the sharp edge of fear replaced by something harder. Determination.

"So, we go in," she says. "We get what we need."

Slater studies her, his gaze searching her face, reading the fire burning just beneath her skin. "You sure you're up for that?"

She meets his eyes without hesitation, something fierce in the way her chin tilts up.

"I'm sure."

"We'll need a plan," Ava says, her voice steady despite the weight of what they're about to do. "A way past security. A way to not be seen."

"And someone watching from the outside," Eli adds, already thinking ahead. His fingers tap restlessly against his laptop as his mind runs through possibilities. "I can do that. Hack into their cameras, maybe. Create a blackout long enough for you to get in and out."

Slater exhales, crossing his arms. "And if we get caught?" He asks the question no one wants to say out loud, always the one thinking about the dangers Piper tries to ignore.

But this time, she doesn't ignore it.

"We don't," Piper says before anyone else can, her voice sharp and final. "We can't."

Silence settles over them, thick and heavy, the enormity of what they're planning sinking into their bones.

Then Ava straightens, her shoulders squared. Determined. Unshaken.

"Okay," she says, glancing around at each of them. "Then let's figure out how to make sure we don't."

Later, as the others head home to start planning, Piper and Slater linger at the foot of her driveway. The sky above them deepens from a dusky purple to an inky blue, stars flickering to life against the darkness. The porch light glows steadily, casting soft pools of gold across the pristine walkway and the neatly trimmed hedges lining the front steps.

Behind her, the house stands tall and polished with its white siding and dark shutters, the kind of place that looks like it belongs in a real estate ad. The windows are spotless, the curtains drawn just right. Everything is in its place. Perfect.

But Piper knows better. Inside, the air is always too still, too pristine, like a museum where no one actually lives. The furniture is expensive but untouched; the kitchen gleams but is rarely used. There's no mess, no clutter—just carefully maintained order that does nothing to fill the silence. The silence from her dad's death.

"You okay?" Slater asks, his voice quiet, careful. He watches her like he already knows the answer.

Piper exhales slowly, watching her breath curl in the crisp night air. "No," she admits. "But I'm not running either."

Slater smiles a mix of pride and sadness all at once. "Good. Because I'm not letting you face this alone."

Something in her chest tightens, but this time, it's not panicking. She reaches out, her fingers brushing against him before twining with his, holding on.

"I'm scared," she whispers.

"Me too," he says, his grip firm, steady. "But I'm more scared of what happens if we don't stop them."

Piper swallows hard, then leans into him,

resting her head against his shoulder.

And for now, with the night stretching quiet around them and Slater solid beside her, it's enough to keep her from breaking.

Chapter 15

The Point of No Return

Ava's house smells like coffee and lemon candles, warm and familiar, but Piper barely registers it. All she can focus on is the plan—the one they're about to lay out like a battle map, every move calculated, every risk measured.

The four of them are crammed around Ava's sleek dining room table, a stark contrast to the chaos that covers it. Laptops glow in front of them, illuminating open documents and blurry security footage. Notes are scribbled in half-legible handwriting across loose sheets of paper, scattered between pizza boxes and half-empty soda cans. A small ceramic dish sits in the center of the table, initially intended for decoration but now repurposed as a catch-all for stray paperclips and crumpled napkins.

Piper leans forward, her elbows on the table, fingers drumming restlessly against her notebook.

Her thoughts are racing too fast, the flood of ideas, fears, and possibilities pressing against her skull.

"Okay," Ava says, pulling up a diagram on her screen, the glow casting sharp lines across her focused expression. "This is the layout of the Whispering Hills Casino's hotel offices."

She turns the laptop so everyone can see, and just like that, the room seems to shrink, the tension pulling tight.

This is it. No more what-ifs. No more backing out. They're doing this.

Slater leans in, squinting at the grainy floor plan Ava somehow dug up because Ava finds everything.

The blueprint is faded, scanned from who-knows-where, but the layout is clear enough. Hallways. Offices. Entrances and exits. It's all there, a puzzle they need to solve before stepping inside the real thing.

Here's the security station," Ava says, pointing to a small, enclosed room near the corner of the layout. "We avoid that at all costs. Cameras are run through there."

Across the table, Eli absently chews on the end of a pencil, eyes flicking between his laptop and the diagram. "I can hack the camera system from outside, like we talked about," he says. "Give you maybe ten minutes of blackout, possibly fifteen if I'm lucky. After that, the system will reset, and they'll know something's up."

"Ten minutes?" Piper echoes, her fingers tightening around her notebook. "That's not a lot of time."

Slater doesn't hesitate. He glances at her, eyes steady, voice firm. "Then we don't waste a second."

His words settle between them like an unspoken vow. They get in. They get proof. They get out.

Ava scrolls to another file, the glow of the screen casting shadows across her face. A list of employees and fake accounts flashes on the monitor. Names already linked to Lasky, proof of something rotten just beneath the surface of the casino's pristine reputation.

"Slater and Piper go in," Ava says, her voice even, but her eyes flick between them with something close to hesitation. "If anyone recognizes me, I'm done. But you two," she pauses, choosing her words carefully, "You're good at being invisible when you need to be."

"Or causing a distraction if it goes south," Eli mutters, smirking as he taps his laptop absently.

Piper raises a brow. "I don't do subtle."

"Exactly," Eli says, grinning. "Which is why, if

you need an exit, cause a scene. I'll start the backup plan."

Slater shifts in his chair, his jaw tightening slightly, fingers tapping against the table in that slow, methodical way Piper recognizes. He's already running through every risk, every worst-case scenario. He always does.

She leans in just slightly, lowering her voice so only he can hear. "I'll need you watching my back."

His gaze meets hers, steady, unwavering.

"Always," he murmurs.

The table falls silent, the kind of silence that isn't empty but heavy. They're thick with the weight of what they're about to do. The glow from their screens flickers across their faces, but no one moves, no one speaks, the reality of the risk settling deep in their bones.

Ava exhales; her voice is quieter now. "If this goes wrong," she says, choosing her words carefully, "Lasky's not the kind of guy who lets people walk away."

Piper swallows hard, her throat tight, the unspoken thought that they might not get another chance hanging between them.

"We know," she says, her voice rough but confident.

Slater leans forward, his fingers laced together,

his gaze steady. "But if we don't do this," he says, his voice calm, but carrying weight, "how many more girls disappear?"

No one has an answer for that.

Because there isn't one.

Later, when they leave Ava's house, Piper and Slater walk slowly down the quiet street, their footsteps the only sound in the thick stillness of the night. Streetlights cast long, stretched-out shadows across the pavement, their glow flickering in places, making everything feel unsteady.

Neither of them speaks at first; both are lost in their thoughts. The weight of what's ahead presses down on them, settling in their bones.

Then, suddenly, Piper stops.

Slater takes another step before realizing she is no longer beside him. He turns, watching her as she stands in the middle of the sidewalk, arms crossed tightly over her chest.

"Are you sure?" she asks, her voice quiet but sharp around the edges. "I mean, you don't have to do this. You don't have to risk it for me."

Slater frowns, his brows pulling together, but he doesn't answer right away. Instead, he steps closer, closing the space between them.

"I'm not doing this for you," he says.

For a split second, her stomach drops until he

keeps talking.

"I'm doing this with you," he says firmly. "Because this is the right thing. Because I care what happens to you. Because I care about that girl, we saw. And because you don't get to carry this alone."

Piper stares at him, chest tight, throat burning.

She doesn't know what to say.

But for the first time in a long time, she doesn't feel like she must.

"You're kinda great, you know that?" Piper whispers, her voice cracking at the edges.

Slater's lips quirk into a small, crooked smile. "Don't tell anyone," He murmurs. "I've got a reputation to maintain."

Piper laughs a genuine laugh, breaking through the weight of the night and shaking something loose in her chest. The sound surprises even her.

And before she can second-guess it, before doubt can creep in, she steps forward and wraps her arms around him.

For a second, Slater freezes, like he wasn't expecting it. Like no one has ever held him like this before. But then his arms come around her, warm and steady, pulling her close.

Piper exhales, sinking into him, her cheek pressing against his shoulder. The tension in her limbs eases slightly as the world quiets around them.

"You've got me," he murmurs against her hair.

Piper tightens her grip, eyes slipping shut.

"I know," she whispers back. "You've got me too."

As they pull back, Piper swipes at her eyes with the sleeve of her hoodie, then smirks, her voice lighter than it has any right to be. "So. You and me. Breaking into a hotel like total criminals."

Slater huffs a quiet laugh, shaking his head. "Guess so." But there's something steady in his smile, like as long as he's doing this with her, it doesn't feel quite so terrifying.

They fall into step beside each other, walking the rest of the way home in silence. But it's not a heavy silence.

It's a promise.

Tomorrow, they'll cross the line. Step into something they can't undo. And there's no turning back.

Chapter 16

Inside the Lion's Den

The back alley behind Whispering Hills Casino feels darker than Piper remembers. The shadows stretch longer and heavier, pooling deep in the cracks of the pavement like they know what's really happening behind these walls. The air smells like cigarette smoke and damp concrete, tinged with the faint, greasy scent of something fried from a nearby dumpster.

Slater stands beside her, his grip firm on his cane but his posture unwavering. The neon glow of the casino sign flickers above them, casting shifting colors against his face: blue, red, gold, like the city itself, can't decide what to make of them.

"You ready?" he asks, his voice quiet but steady.

Piper swallows hard and looks up at the glowing sign, its letters humming, its promise of luxury and luck, nothing but a front for something so much worse. Her pulse pounds against her ribs, fast and insistent.

"Not even a little," she mutters.

Then she exhales, squares her shoulders, and takes a step forward.

"Let's go."

Ava's instructions had been clear, "There's a service entrance by the loading docks. The door's got a faulty lock—my mom said you can jiggle it open if you're careful."

Now, standing in the alley beside the rusted metal door, Piper can feel her pulse in her fingertips, thrumming like a warning. The night hums around them, muffled music from inside, the distant screech of tires on wet pavement, the faint buzz of a flickering neon sign down the street.

She glances at Slater. "You good?"

"Yeah," he says, but his knuckles are white where they grip his cane.

Piper doesn't push it. She just reaches for the handle, fingers curling around the cold metal. She jiggles it, just like Ava said, her breath shallow as the lock resists for a second, then clicks. Just like that, they're in.

The hallway inside is dim and narrow, with all industrial grays and exposed pipes. The walls are streaked with old water stains and the air reeks of bleach and cigarette smoke. A staff-only sign hangs crooked on the wall, its edges peeling.

"Okay," Slater murmurs, scanning their surroundings. "Ava said the back offices are on the third floor, right?"

Piper nods, swallowing against the dryness in her throat. "Elevator?"

"Risky."

"Stairs?"

"Riskier," he admits, smirking weakly. "But less likely to get caught on camera."

Piper exhales sharply, then jerks her chin toward the door at the end of the hall.

The stairwell.

Without another word, they slip inside, closing the door behind them. The air is cooler here, the silence heavier.

Piper moves first, stepping carefully, her shoes barely making a sound against the concrete steps. Behind her, Slater follows, moving with quiet determination, his grip on the railing tightening as he pushes forward.

She keeps her pace steady, casting quick glances over her shoulder, her heart hammering.

They can't get caught. They won't get caught. They don't have another choice.

By the time they reach the third floor, Piper's pulse is a wild, unrelenting drumbeat in her ears. She swears it's loud enough to give them away.

The hallway stretches before them, long and sterile, lined with dull gray doors and flickering fluorescent lights that cast a cold, washed-out glow. The air is thick with the scent of old carpet and stale coffee, an eerie contrast to the weight of what they're about to do.

They stop in front of a heavy office door, its

surface scratched and dented with years of use. A bold red sign reads AUTHORIZED PERSONNEL ONLY.

"This is it," Piper whispers, her voice barely more than a breath.

Slater glances around, scanning for anything they missed. "Cameras?"

Piper follows his gaze, her stomach tightening. The hallway is lined with them, little black domes tucked into the corners, but Eli's blackout seems to be holding as the small red indicator lights are currently off. But it won't last forever.

Slater grips the handle, testing it. Locked.

Piper exhales sharply, digging into her pocket. Her fingers close around a bobby pin, cool against her skin, and she pulls it free. Her hands tremble as she crouches, sliding it into the lock, the tiny click of metal against metal almost deafening in the quiet.

Slater leans down slightly, whispering just behind her. "You've done this before?" His voice is low, edged with quiet amusement despite the thick tension in the air.

Piper smirks, even as panic claws at her ribs. "Don't ask."

Then she twists the pin, holding her breath—

And the lock gives with a soft snick. The door swings open. They slip inside.

The office is far nicer than Piper expected. Not the sterile, corporate kind of nice, but the kind that screams money: the kind meant to intimidate. The walls are lined with dark mahogany shelves, filled more with expensive-looking décor than actual books. A polished wood desk sits in the center, sleek and powerful, its surface pristine except for a single glass of amber liquid, still half-full.

To the right, a bar gleams under dim lighting, stocked with bottles that probably cost more than her mom makes in a month. The scent of expensive cologne and old cigars lingers in the air, a stark contrast to the sweat prickling at the back of Piper's neck.

But it's the file cabinet in the corner that makes her blood run cold. Unlike everything else in the office, it's a plain, gray metal, utilitarian, and out of place among the luxury. And locked. Because whatever's inside isn't meant to be seen.

Slater moves to the door without a word, his posture rigid, every muscle alert. His fingers tighten around his cane as he listens, his head tilting slightly like he's catching every distant sound. "I'll listen. You look."

Piper nods, swallowing hard. Then she drops to her knees in front of the cabinet, her pulse thudding as she yanks open the top drawer.

Piper's breath catches as she flips open the first file. Inside, there are ledgers. Rows and rows of names and numbers scrawled in careful handwriting, the ink bleeding slightly on the aged paper. Then, the photos.

Stacks of them, clipped to documents, faces staring back at her. Different girls, some older, some terrifyingly young. Some Piper recognizes.

Her stomach twists violently as she traces her fingers over one in particular: a girl from a missing person's flyer at the grocery store. The one taped next to the register, the one with hopeful blue eyes and a date stamped under her name. Missing since last August.

She flips to another. Then another.

Payments are tracked beside their names, which display huge amounts and unsettling numbers; some are circled, while others have strange initials scribbled next to them. Transactions. Proof.

Her hands shake as she moves through the pages, "Oh my God," she whispers, her voice barely audible over the rush of blood in her ears.

Slater turns sharply. "What?"

Piper swallows hard, feeling like her entire body is vibrating. "They're all here," she says, her voice tight, strained. "All the girls. Everything he's done."

Slater's jaw clenches, his expression going from shock to something harder. Something colder. "Get photos. Now."

Piper fumbles for her phone, her fingers trembling as she snaps shot after shot, her pulse pounding with every click of the shutter.

They have proof.

But now, they must get out.

Just as Piper snaps the last photo, the sound cuts through the silence. Footsteps. Heavy. Sharp. Coming closer.

Slater's eyes widen, alarm flashing across his face. "Someone's coming."

Piper freezes, her breath catching in her throat.

Slater doesn't hesitate. He moves, grabbing her wrist and yanking her behind the office door just as a key scrapes into the lock.

The door swings open.

Piper holds her breath, pressing herself against the wall, Slater's grip firm around her wrist, grounding her.

Lasky. He steps inside, his expensive shoes clicking against the polished floor, his movements brisk, oblivious. He walks straight to the desk, dropping a folder onto its surface with a dull thud, his phone pressed to his ear.

"Yeah, everything's ready for tonight," he mutters, distracted. "The new girl will be gone before anyone asks questions."

Piper's stomach flips, bile rising in her throat.

"No, it's handled. The kid poking around won't be a problem much longer."

Slater's hand tightens around her wrist, his grip just shy of painful.

She doesn't need to look at him to know.

Lasky is talking about them.

Lasky turns toward the bar, his back to the door, as he pours himself a drink; the ice clinks softly against the glass. His posture is relaxed, completely unaware that two people are frozen just feet away, listening to every word.

Slater leans in, his breath warm against Piper's ear as he whispers, so quietly she barely catches it, "Now."

They are moving. Slipping out in a silent blur, stepping carefully, closing the door without a sound.

Lasky's phone rings again just as they make it into the hallway, his voice fading behind them. Piper doesn't dare look back. They walk fast but quietly, each step calculated, pushing toward the stairwell as if their lives depended on it because they do.

By the time they reach the alley, the night air is a slap to the face: cold, sharp, real. Piper staggers, her hand catching the rough brick wall as her knees threaten to give out.

Slater isn't much better, breathing hard, leaning heavily on his cane, his face tight with exhaustion.

For a moment, neither of them speaks.

Then, "Okay," Piper gasps, her voice shaky but alive. "Okay. We got it."

Slater lets out a breathless laugh, a grin spreading across his face that's wide, wild, real.

"Yeah," he says, chest still heaving. "We did."

As they walk away, the neon glow of the Whispering Hills Casino fading behind them, Slater glances over at Piper.

"You good?" he asks, his voice quieter now, the adrenaline still buzzing between them.

Piper exhales, shaking her head, but a slow, determined smile still tugs at her lips. "Not even close." She looks up at him, eyes steady, voice stronger than it should be after everything. "But I've never been this sure about anything in my life."

Slater's smile mirrors hers, which is small but unwavering, carrying the weight of everything they've just done, everything they still have to do.

Without thinking, Piper reaches for his hand.

Without hesitation, he takes it.

"We take them down," she says, her grip firm, her eyes burning with fire.

Slater squeezes her hand, nodding once, "Yeah," he says. "We take them down."

Together.

Chapter 17

Cracks in the Armor

Piper's room is dim, the only light spilling from a lamp in the corner, its golden glow stretching long shadows across the walls.

She shuts the door softly behind Slater, the quiet click of the lock sealing them away from the outside world as if she needs a barrier—something solid, something certain.

For a long moment, silence settles between them, thick and heavy.

Slater leans back against the wall, chest rising and falling in uneven breaths. Sweat glistens at his temple, catching the low light.

Piper tosses her sketchbook onto the bed, the

pages fluttering before it lands. Then, she starts pacing, her fingers threading through her hair, tugging as though she can unravel the chaos in her head if she pulls hard enough.

When Piper turns to speak, the words catch in her throat because Slater is pale, his knuckles white where they grip the edge of her dresser like it's the only thing keeping him upright.

"Slater?" Her voice is sharp, cutting through the haze of her thoughts. Everything else falls away.

He tries to wave her off with a weak flick of his fingers, but it's useless as she's already moving. She barely reaches him before his legs give out, and he sinks to the floor, his cane slipping from his grasp and clattering against the hardwood.

"I'm fine," he grits out, but his body betrays him. His leg trembles violently, muscles seizing, and she knows better.

"No, you're not." She drops to her knees in front of him, her hands firm on his shoulders, steadying him. Her gaze sharpens all the frantic energy from before, narrowing into one clear focus:

him. "You should've told me you were hurting."

His jaw clenches, frustration flickering behind his exhaustion. "Didn't want to screw it up. We needed to do this."

Piper exhales, the breath unsteady, as she reaches out to smooth, damp strands of hair from his forehead. Her touch is gentle and deliberate. "You didn't screw up anything," she says softly. "You're the reason we got out of there."

Slater leans his head back against the dresser, his chest rising and falling in uneven breaths. For a moment, he doesn't speak. Then, in a voice barely above a whisper, he finally admits, "It hurts. It hasn't hurt this bad in a while."

The words cut through her, sharp and aching.

"Okay," she says, grounding herself, grounding him. "Then we sit. We breathe. You don't have to be strong for me right now, okay?"

His gaze lifts to hers, and something in it softens at the fierceness in her eyes, at the unwavering way she stays beside him.

A moment passes. Then, he exhales. "Yeah,"

he murmurs. "Okay."

They sit in silence, the weight of everything settling around them, until Piper starts tapping restless fingers against her thigh. Her eyes dart too fast, scanning the room like she's searching for an escape hatch.

"Piper," Slater says gently.

"I'm fine," she cuts in, too quick, too bright. Before he can respond, she's on her feet, pacing in tight, frantic strides. "We did it. We got what we needed. It's good. It's all good."

But her breathing tells a different story: too fast, too shallow. Her mind is running, spinning, caught in a loop she can't break.

"We're gonna take them down, Slater," she says, her voice sharp, crackling with something electric, something dangerous. Her eyes gleam, too bright, too wild. "We're gonna burn it all down."

Slater watches her carefully, reading between every line, every sharp edge. He's seen this before. He knows where it leads.

"Piper," he says again, softer now like he's

coaxing a bird away from a window before it crashes. "Sit down."

"I can't," she snaps, her voice fraying at the edges. "If I sit, I'll think too much and."

She cuts herself off, shaking her head hard like she can shake away the spiral tightening in her chest.

"Hey," Slater says, reaching for her hand, his fingers warm and steady against hers. "Look at me."

She does, but her eyes are too wide, too wild; her chest rises and falls in shallow, uneven breaths.

"You're okay," he murmurs, his voice quiet, grounding. "You're here. You don't have to carry all of this right now."

Her lip quivers, her grip tightening around him like it's the only thing keeping her tethered. "But if I stop moving, Slater, I'm gonna fall apart."

He doesn't hesitate. "Then I'll catch you."

She stares at him, her whole body humming with restless, unspent energy, like a live wire sparking in the dark.

Then, slowly, like moving through water, she lowers herself to the floor beside him. Her back presses against the dresser, her limbs feeling heavier with every inch she sinks down. And then, finally, she lets her head tip against his shoulder.

Slater doesn't hesitate. His arm comes around her, instinctive and steady, pulling her in like an anchor.

"Just breathe with me," he murmurs, his voice low, soothing. He sets the rhythm, slow and measured, like a quiet metronome.

At first, her breaths are uneven, catching in her throat, but she tries. She focuses on the warmth of his arm, the steady rise and fall of his chest, the quiet, constant beat of his heart.

Piper's bedroom is a world of its own, dimly lit, with walls covered in charcoal sketches and half-finished paintings; the air is thick with the scent of dried acrylic and graphite. A cluttered desk sits beneath the glow of a string of fairy lights, their golden hue casting soft halos over scattered brushes, paint-stained rags, and a forgotten cup of cold tea. Sketchbooks pile at the foot of her bed, some open, their pages filled with frantic strokes and raw emotion.

She presses her back against the dresser, her voice barely more than a whisper, raw and frayed. "I hate this. I hate feeling like my brain's gonna break."

Slater exhales beside her, his hand still loosely wrapped around hers. "I hate this too. The pain, the feeling like I'm not whole anymore."

She lifts her head, searching his face, their eyes locking like two storm fronts meeting, both carrying too much weight. However, in that connection, in the quiet understanding that stretches between them, there is something solid. Something real.

"But we're still here," Piper says softly.

Slater nods, his grip is just a little firmer. "Yeah. We are."

They sit there, shoulder to shoulder, as the weight of everything slowly shifts, settling into something quieter, something bearable. Their breathing evens out, syncing with the steady hum of the world outside, cars passing in the distance, and the soft creak of the old furniture and house settling around them.

Piper's gaze drifts around her room, taking in the scattered remnants of herself: the half-finished paintings leaning against the wall, their colors streaked with frustration; the battered sketchbooks stacked haphazardly on the floor, pages curling at the edges from use. A cluster of charcoal pencils sits forgotten on her desk, dusted in black smudges. String lights drape across the ceiling, their dim glow casting long, golden shadows that make the space feel smaller and safer.

"I'm gonna be okay," she says at last, the words tentative but real.

Slater's eyes move over her work: art filled with raw emotion, the kind that spills out when words won't do. He nods. "You are."

She turns her head, meeting his gaze. "And so are you."

A faint smile tugs at his lips. "Not if I keep climbing three flights of stairs for you."

Piper lets out a soft laugh, the sound warm and genuine. She tilts her head onto his shoulder, exhaustion pulling at the edges of her body, but something lighter settling in her chest. "Guess we're stuck with each other now."

"Guess so."

For a long while, neither of them moves. The world outside keeps turning, but here, in this space, surrounded by messy sketches, broken-in paintbrushes, and the lingering scent of turpentine, they just exist.

Maybe they don't have all the answers yet. Maybe their bodies and minds are still waging battles, and neither of them fully understands. But for now, at this moment, they're not fighting alone.

Chapter 18

Lines in the Sand

By the time Piper and Slater return to Ava's house, the adrenaline has burned away, leaving something colder and heavier in its place. The weight of what they now carry inside Piper's phone.

Ava's living room is a controlled kind of chaos. The scent of stale coffee and too many energy drinks lingers in the air, mingling with the faint aroma of lavender from the candle still flickering on the windowsill. Papers are scattered across the coffee table; some are crumpled from frustration, others marked with hurried notes and diagrams. Two open laptops sit on the floor, their screens casting a bluish glow against the dim room. Empty energy drink cans are stacked haphazardly beside them, a monument to how long Ava and Eli have been at this.

When Piper and Slater step inside, Ava is on her feet in an instant, her sharp eyes scanning them, already reading between the lines, already knowing. Something big happened.

"You got it?" she asks, her voice tight with urgency.

Piper doesn't answer. She moves past her, drops onto the couch with a heavy sigh, and pulls out her phone. Without a word, she hands it to Ava.

And just like that, the air in the room shifts—no more waiting, no more hoping. Now, it's real.

Ava settles back onto the floor; the glow from her laptop screen reflects in her tense expression as she opens the files, scrolling through the images with methodical precision. The blue light sharpens the set of her jaw, the way her mouth presses into a thin line. The room is quiet except for the faint hum of the computers and the occasional rustling of papers as Eli shifts beside her.

Slater lowers himself onto the armrest next to Piper, moving carefully, his muscles still protesting from the strain of the night. He doesn't say anything—watches, his expression unreadable, but his fingers grip the couch cushion a little too tightly.

"You're kidding me," Eli mutters after barely thirty seconds of scrolling, his voice tinged with disbelief and something darker.

Ava exhales sharply, her eyes flicking over the screen. "These are girls," she says softly, the words heavy, sickening. "All of them. Names, fake IDs, dates, and amounts paid for them."

Piper stares at the flickering candle on the windowsill, the scent of lavender suddenly cloying, suffocating. She swallows hard. "And there's more," she says, voice flat. "Some of them are local. Some of them are girls we've seen on missing posters."

Ava's head snaps up, eyes sharp, burning. "This is bigger than just Lasky," she says, gripping the laptop like she could crush it in her hands. "He's not working alone."

Slater nods grimly. "Yeah. And if we go to the

cops with this before we know who else is involved, it could disappear."

The air in the room tightens like all the oxygen has been sucked out.

Eli keeps scrolling, his brows furrowed, his jaw clenched. "Cops might be on his payroll. Or someone higher up. If Savannah's dad is bankrolling this..."

Piper barely breathes, her heart pounding in her ears. "Then it's not just Lasky we have to worry about."

For a long moment, the only sounds in the room are the low hum of Ava's laptop, the faint ticking of the wall clock, and the distant rumble of a car passing outside. The air is thick, weighted with the enormity of what they've just uncovered, pressing down on all of them.

It's Ava who finally breaks the silence, "So, what do we do now?" she asks softly. But her voice isn't hesitant; instead, it's razor-sharp, edged with resolve, her hands curling into fists against her knees. She's ready for a fight.

Slater glances at Piper, waiting for her to decide if she'll be the one to answer.

Piper feels the weight of their eyes on her. But for the first time, it doesn't make her want to shrink or run. It roots her. Grounds her.

She lifts her head, her jaw tightening as she meets their gazes.

"We don't stop," she says, her voice steady, unwavering. "We keep going until we have everything. Enough to take down all of them."

Ava nods slowly, a fierce spark igniting in her expression.

Eli hesitates, his fingers still resting on the laptop trackpad, the screen's cold glow washing over his face. "And what if we don't have time?" he asks. "What if they find out what we have before we're ready?"

The room seems to shrink around them, the walls lined with half-drunk coffee cups, scattered papers, and the quiet, suffocating awareness that they're up against something much bigger than any of them.

The room is a mess of late nights and desperation, like half-eaten chip bags crumpled beside empty coffee cups and granola bar wrappers strewn across the table like discarded evidence of their exhaustion. Papers are spread haphazardly over the floor, some dog-eared, others covered in frantic notes and crossed-out plans. The air is thick with the scent of stale caffeine, lavender wax melting from that nearly finished flickering candle on the windowsill, and the unmistakable tension pressing in from all sides.

Slater shifts, rubbing the back of his neck, his voice quiet but heavy. "About that."

Ava's head snaps up, eyes sharp.

"We got a message yesterday. A photo of us. Watching us."

The words settle like a stone in the center of the room.

Ava's breath hitches, her knuckles tightening around the edge of her laptop. "What?"

Eli curses under his breath, running a hand through his already messy hair. His foot nudges an empty Red Bull can, sending it rolling softly across the hardwood floor. "So, they know someone's poking around."

"Yeah," Slater confirms, his gaze flicking to Piper, unreadable. "They know."

Eli leans forward, elbows braced against his knees, his fingers tapping restlessly against the fabric of his jeans. The glow from the laptop screen flickers across his face, casting sharp shadows beneath his eyes. Papers are scattered across the coffee table in front of him; some are smudged with fingerprints, others creased from being handled too many times.

"So, we've got two options," he says, voice low but firm. "One, we go to the cops now, risk losing it all if someone in the department is dirty. Two, we get more, tie it straight to Savannah's dad, and blow the whole thing up ourselves."

The silence stretches between them. The candle on the windowsill has burned low, wax dripping down its side in slow, uneven trails.

"And three," Piper says, her voice cutting

through the quiet like a blade. "We do nothing. Stay quiet. Pretend we don't know what we know."

All three of them look at her.

Slater shifts beside her, his voice softer but just as firm. "But if we do that, more girls will disappear. You know that."

Piper nods, her jaw clenched so tightly it aches. "I know."

Eli studies her, his expression unreadable. "So, what's it gonna be?"

Piper lets her gaze sweep around the room: the tangled cords from too many all-nighters, the kitten playing with the crushed granola bar wrapper on the floor, the open laptop humming with everything they've uncovered. She looks at Ava, sitting rigid but resolute, her eyes gleaming with quiet determination. At Eli, a smirk but a serious expression beneath it. At Slater, steady as ever, an anchor in the storm.

She exhales, slow and deliberate.

"We go all in," she says finally. "We get enough to make sure no one can bury this. We don't back down."

Ava straightens, her fingers drumming against her laptop as the glow of the screen illuminates the determination on her face. "Okay," she says, her voice firm, slicing through the heavy air. "First, we need to find out who else is involved. If it's Savannah's dad, there's probably more. People at the top, protecting him. City council, cops, maybe even casino owners."

The room remains a mess from late-night desperation. The kitten is not peeking out from half-eaten party-size chip bags, stacks of crumpled notes, and energy drink cans shoved aside on the coffee table. The candle on the windowsill has nearly burned itself out, a pool of melted wax creeping down its side.

Eli leans back against the couch, running a hand through his hair, eyes sharp with focus. "I can try to dig into bank records, property ownership to see who's moving money to Lasky."

Ava nods. "And I can start watching the hotel. Who comes and goes. What girls are being brought in."

Piper's stomach twists at that, bile rising at the thought of what watching really means, like seeing it happen in real-time, knowing they can't stop it yet. But she forces herself to nod.

"Good," she says, swallowing against the unease. "And we need a way to get this out when we're ready like something public, something huge."

Slater is watching her, his expression unreadable for a second. Then, something shifts, something fierce, something unshakable.

"We'll figure that out," he says, and there's no hesitation in his voice. No doubt. Just the quiet, steady certainty that whatever comes next, they're in this together.

The living room is cluttered with the remnants of a life that doesn't quite fit the chaos of what they're planning. Framed family photos hang on the walls of Ava and her parents at a beach, a younger version of her in a soccer uniform, and an old black-and-white picture of her grandparents. Wooden shelves line one side of the room, filled with mismatched knick-knacks and souvenirs from road trips, dusty paperbacks, and a ceramic owl with a chip in its wing. A crocheted blanket, probably made by Ava's grandmother, is draped over the back of the couch, worn soft from use.

As they start tossing out ideas and making lists, the weight of it all settles into Piper's bones. The fire in her chest is real, but underneath it, a slight tremor of fear lingers, coiling tight.

She glances at Slater, and the moment their eyes meet, he gives her a small, knowing smile as he can already hear the thoughts racing through her head before she even says a word.

"We've got this," he murmurs, voice steady, grounding. "You've got this."

She nods, but as she leans back against the couch, the weight of everything presses in around her. The soft cushions feel out of place beneath her, as if they're too normal, too safe for the war they're about to step into.

Because even if they win, if they expose everything and burn it all down, what happens to people like them? What's left? But maybe that doesn't matter. Perhaps the fight is worth it anyway.

As they huddle around Ava's laptop, the screen casting a cool glow over their faces, the room feels smaller, like it's crowded with urgency, with determination, with something that feels dangerously close to hope. Papers are spread across the coffee table, filled with half-scribbled notes and strategies, overlapping like pieces of a puzzle they're still trying to solve. The scent of stale coffee lingers in the air, mixing with the faint traces of Ava's mom's lavender-scented candle.

Piper glances around. At Ava, her eyes are sharp and calculating as she types, fingers flying over the keyboard. At Eli, slouched but alert, tossing out ideas with a smirk that doesn't quite mask the seriousness in his eyes. At Slater, steady beside her, his presence solid, unshakable.

And then it hits her. She's not alone. Not anymore. The realization settles deep, anchoring her. The weight of everything hasn't lifted; it's still there, pressing at the edges of her mind, whispering all the ways this could go wrong. But for the first time since this whole thing started, that weight is shared. And for now, that feels like enough.

Chapter 19

First Blood

The plan was simple. Or at least, it had seemed simple in theory.

Piper stands tucked in the shadow of a closed storefront, the "For Lease" sign peeling in the dirty window behind her. The air is thick with the scent of city dust and car exhaust, the pavement beneath her feet still warm from the sun that had set hours ago. A flickering street lamp hums overhead, casting a shaky light onto the cracked sidewalk.

Across the street, Savannah's dad steps out of a sleek black SUV, the polished surface reflecting the neon buzz of a nearby diner sign. He adjusts his tie with the practiced ease of a man who thinks he owns the world, his gaze sweeping the street as if he has already dismissed everything in it. Another important meeting in a town already crumbling at its edges.

Piper tugs her hoodie lower, her pulse a steady drumbeat against her ribs. Her fingers tighten around her phone, ready to snap a photo, to call for help, or to run, if it comes to that.

"Target on the move," she murmurs into her earbuds, keeping her voice low.

"You don't have to say it like we're in a spy movie," Eli mutters back, but there's an edge to his voice, tensc, focused. He knows this is real.

Further down the street, Slater leans casually against a lamppost, hands in his pockets, looking like just another guy out for a late-night walk. But Piper knows better. He's watching. Waiting. Ready.

Her eyes flick to him, and when he meets her gaze across the street, something in her steadies. The fear doesn't disappear, but it shifts, settling into something sharper, something more potent.

With him here, with all of them in this, she's

not just afraid.

She's ready.

Savannah's dad moves fast, his polished shoes clicking against the pavement with purpose, but Piper moves faster. She slips through the shadows, darting behind parked cars and weaving through alleyways with a kind of instinct she never realized she had. The city around her hums with late-night energy like distant sirens, muffled music from a bar down the block, and the occasional flicker of movement from an apartment window above.

She stays close but careful, her breath controlled, her hands steady as she watches him turn down a quieter street, heading toward a building she's never noticed before.

It's upscale: too nice for this part of town. Sleek glass doors and tinted windows reveal nothing inside. A discreet gold plaque by the entrance, the kind of place that doesn't need a name because the people who matter already know it.

Piper ducks behind a mailbox, pressing herself into the shadows. "Ava," she whispers, barely moving her lips. "You getting this?"

A second later, Ava's voice crackles in her earbuds, calm and steady as ever. "Yeah. That's a private business front. But from what I'm pulling up now, it's owned by one of Lasky's companies."

Piper's stomach twists. She stares at the building, her pulse pounding in her ears. "This is it," she mutters, her grip on her phone tightening.

Piper moves to follow again, slipping from shadow to shadow, but something makes her glance back to check on Slater.

And immediately, she knows something's off.

He's gripping his cane too tightly, his knuckles white around the handle. His face is pale under the weak glow of the streetlamp, and his jaw clenches like he's holding back something more than just exhaustion.

Her stomach twists.

"Slater," she says softly, her voice barely above a whisper. "You good?"

"I'm fine," he grits out, but she sees the way he's swaying, the uneven shift in his stance. The way he's breathing too hard, too shallow.

"No, you're not," she says, panic coiling in her chest.

"I've got this," he insists. But when he takes a step forward to follow her, his leg gives out.

Piper's heart drops.

"Slater!" she hisses, lunging back just in time to catch him before he collapses. His weight leans heavily against her, his breath warm but unsteady against her shoulder.

"I just pushed too hard," he mutters, frustration laced in every syllable as he hates himself for it.

Piper doesn't hesitate. She cups his face, fingers pressing against the sharp angles of his jaw, forcing him to meet her eyes. "You don't have to do this like you're indestructible."

He swallows hard, something raw flickering in his expression. "I can't let you do this alone."

"You're not," she says fiercely. "But I need you to not destroy yourself trying to be my hero."

For a long moment, they stare at each other,

the city humming quietly around them. And in the space between words, everything unsaid hangs heavy in the air, loud, undeniable.

Piper steadies Slater as he lowers himself onto the curb, his breathing still uneven, his fingers curled tightly around his cane. The night air feels heavier now, pressing against her skin, but before she can tell him just to breathe, the low purr of an expensive engine draws her attention.

A sleek black car glides down the street, its headlights cutting sharp beams through the dim glow of the street lamps.

Something cold slides down Piper's spine.

The car slows.

Her pulse quickens as the tinted window rolls down—just a few inches, just enough for her to catch a glimpse of his sharp, calculating gaze. Lasky.

His eyes are unreadable, but his smirk is razor-sharp, all slow amusement wrapped in something much darker.

"Nice night for a walk," he murmurs, voice smooth, almost lazy, but the mockery is thick beneath it.

Piper stiffens, her hand tightening around Slater's arm, her nails digging into his sleeve.

"Stay away from us," she grits out, her voice low, dangerous.

Lasky chuckles, a rich, empty sound like they're just two kids playing pretend, and he's already decided how this ends. He shakes his head, almost pitying them.

"Careful, kids," he says lightly. "You're playing a game you don't understand. People get hurt when they don't know when to stop."

The window rolls up. The car pulls away, the engine's purr fading into the night.

But the silence it leaves behind is thick. Smothering. A threat wrapped in velvet.

Slater exhales, the breath shaky, uneven. His gaze stays locked on the spot where the car disappeared, his jaw tight, his grip white-knuckled around his cane.

"He knows," he murmurs, his voice barely above a breath. "He knows exactly what we're doing."

Piper swallows hard, heat coiling in her chest, a slow-burning fury settling beneath her ribs. Her hands curl into fists, nails pressing into her palms. Let him know. Let him see.

"Good," she says, her voice sharp, unwavering. "Let him watch. He'll see how this ends."

But even as the words leave her lips, even as she tries to hold onto the fire burning within her, something cold slips through the cracks, the weight of it, the reality of what they're up against.

Without thinking, she reaches for Slater's hand, needing something real, something steady. He doesn't hesitate. His fingers close around hers, firm despite the slight tremor in them. He squeezes once, grounding her. She squeezes back.

And in the quiet, between the lingering echoes of the threat left behind, they hold on.

By the time Piper and Slater step through Ava's front door, the weight of the night clings to them like a second skin. The living room is dim, the glow of laptop screens casting eerie blue light over Eli and Ava's tense faces. Empty coffee cups sit forgotten on the cluttered table, a Red Bull can crushed in Eli's hand.

The second Ava takes in Piper's pale face and the unsteady way Slater moves, she's on her feet.

"What happened?" she demands, her sharp eyes flicking between them.

Piper exhales, the words clipped and edged with exhaustion. "Lasky. He saw us. Spoke to us. Threatened us."

Eli mutters a curse under his breath, jaw tightening. "So, he knows we're coming for him."

"Good," Piper snaps, her eyes burning despite the fatigue in her limbs. "Let him be scared."

Ava doesn't look convincing. She glances between them, concern softening the sharp lines of her expression. "But we have to be smart. If he knows, he's going to hit back hard."

Then, her gaze flicks to Slater, her voice quieter. "And Slater?"

"I'm fine," Slater says immediately, straightening despite his body's protests.

Piper cuts him a look. A look that says he's absolutely not fine.

Ava nods slightly, understanding, but doesn't push.

Piper exhales, her voice lower now but still carrying that same heat. That same defiance. "We need a real plan. Before someone gets hurt."

Later, after Eli and Ava bury themselves in work, securing the files and checking for any sign that they're being watched, Piper settles beside Slater on the well-worn sofa. The room is quieter now, the tension dulled but still present, lingering in the hum of the laptops and the occasional hushed conversation across the room.

She presses a cold-water bottle into his hand.

"You scared me today," she whispers.

Slater glances at her, his fingers tightening around the plastic, the guilt evident in his eyes. "Didn't mean to."

"I know."

She exhales, then leans her head against his shoulder. He's tense for half a second, but then she feels him exhaling, his body softening under the weight of her.

"Just don't do that again, okay?" Her voice is quiet, edged with something raw. "Don't think you have to prove something to me."

He nods, his fingers tracing the condensation on the bottle absently. "I won't. But I'm still in this with you. All the way."

Piper closes her eyes for a moment, letting the words settle between them, heavy and unshakable.

"I know," she murmurs. "That's why I'm scared."

They sit like that, surrounded by the distant hum of the city outside, the quiet chaos of a world closing in on them.

But here, at this moment, it's just them.

Two broken kids, ready to fight monsters.

Together.

Chapter 20

The Weight We Carry Too

The room is silent after Piper and Slater leave, but it's not the kind of quiet that soothes. It lingers, heavy and restless, filling the space with something unspoken, something suffocating.

Ava sits at the kitchen table, her fingers curled around a half-empty mug of cold coffee. The glow of her laptop screen illuminates her face, casting sharp shadows under her eyes. The files are still open, with rows of damning evidence laid bare in front of her like an open wound that won't stop bleeding. Every name, every transaction, every photo feels like a weight pressing against her ribs.

A few feet away, Eli sits on the floor, his back against the couch, knees drawn up. His earbuds dangle loosely around his neck, unplugged, silent. A can of Red Bull sits untouched beside him, condensation pooling around the base. His fingers drum against his knee—restless, but his mind is somewhere else, stuck in the gravity of what they've stepped into.

Neither of them speaks. Because what is there to say? They both feel the weight of something too big, too dangerous. The point of no return.

Ava runs her fingers lightly over the laptop keys, tracing them without pressing down. The screen glows in front of her, waiting, urging her to keep going, to dig deeper, to find more, but her chest feels too tight like an invisible band is cinching around her ribs, pulling tighter with every breath.

"You okay?" Eli's voice is softer than usual, cutting through the heavy silence.

She doesn't look up. Her fingers are still.

"I don't know."

Eli shifts where he sits on the floor, pulling his knees closer to his chest. The light from the laptop flickers against the side of his face, catching on the tension in his jaw.

"Yeah. Same."

Ava swallows hard. Her throat burns, her eyes sting, but she won't let it spill over.

She stares at the screen, at the files open like an accusation, like proof that they've crossed a line they can't uncross.

"I thought we could just help a little," she whispers, the words barely escaping the lump in her throat. "Find some information, pass it along. Not—" She gestures toward the screen, toward the names, faces, and horrors staring back at her.

"Not this."

Eli leans back against the couch, tilting his head up, eyes tracing invisible patterns in the ceiling. The dim light from Ava's laptop flickers against his face, casting long shadows under his eyes.

"I know," he says, his voice is quieter than usual. "I thought it was gonna be a game. Like, hacking into stuff, finding dirt on people. Like I was good at something for once."

Ava finally looks over at him, drawn by the rawness in his tone.

Eli isn't the type of person who shows his feelings. He's always smirking, cracking jokes, keeping everything at arm's length. But right now, there's no smirk, no deflection.

Right now, he looks tired. Like all the weight Piper and Slater are carrying has settled onto him, too. Like it's pressing down on his chest, and for once, he doesn't have a clever remark to shove it away.

Ava's fingers curl into the fabric of her hoodie, gripping it like it might hold her together. She stares at the open laptop, at the rows of names and numbers: the proof of something too enormous, too monstrous. The weight of it presses against her ribs, making it hard to breathe.

"What if we can't stop them?" she whispers, her voice barely more than a breath. "What if we're too small?"

Eli doesn't answer right away. The silence stretches between them, thick and unsteady. He stares up at the ceiling, his expression unreadable, as if he's sorting through something in his mind.

Finally, he exhales.

"Then we do it anyway," he says. "Even if it's stupid. Even if we lose."

Ava lets out a shaky breath. Her eyes burn, but she won't let the tears fall. "Why?"

Eli turns his head, meeting her gaze. He holds it, steady and unshaken, for a long moment.

"Because someone has to."

Ava looks away, blinking rapidly, forcing the sting behind her eyes to stay in place.

"My mom worked at that hotel," she says, her voice quiet, almost distant. She traces the edge of her laptop with her fingers, the glow of the screen reflecting in her glassy stare. "She cleaned those rooms. She used to say weird things—like how some girls stayed in the nice suites but never left through the lobby. I didn't get it back then."

Eli is watching her now, his usual easygoing expression replaced with something sharper, more focused.

"And now?" he asks, his voice careful, measured.

Ava swallows hard. "Now I wonder if she knew more than she let on."

The confession settles between them like a weight pressing down on the room, wrapping around the air, thick and suffocating.

Eli's smirk is gone now, stripped away, replaced with something fierce. Something unshakable. He sits up straighter, shoulders squared.

"We'll stop them, Ava," he says, the certainty in his voice cutting through the uncertainty in hers. "We will."

She exhales slowly, forcing a weak smile, but there's something different in her eyes now. A flicker of something real.

"I hope so."

Eli drags a hand through his hair, exhaling sharply. His fingers linger at the back of his neck, as if he's trying to ease some of the tension knotting there.

"You know," he mutters, voice low, "everyone thinks I'm this cocky hacker guy, like I don't care about anything. But I do. I care way too much, and it sucks."

Ava turns toward him and really looks at him. Not just the sarcastic smirk he wears like armor but the exhaustion in his eyes, the weight in his shoulders, and the way his hands fidget when he's not typing. She sees the cracks he never lets anyone else see.

"You don't have to act like it's all a joke around us," she says, her voice gentle but certain.

Eli glances away, his jaw tightening for a second before he swallows. His fingers drum absently against his knee.

"Yeah," he murmurs. "I'm starting to figure that out."

They sit in silence for a moment, but this time, it isn't heavy. It isn't suffocating. It's softer, easier, like for the first time in a while, they're not carrying all of this alone.

The laptop hums quietly on the table, casting a dim glow over Ava's face, over the mess of notes and empty coffee cups scattered between them. The world outside still feels dangerous, still feels too big, but here, in this small pocket of quiet, it's just them.

"You're good at this, Eli," Ava says after a beat. "Not just hacking. You've got our backs. Piper's. Slater's. Mine."

Eli blinks like he wasn't expecting that. Like the words hit a part of him, he wasn't ready to acknowledge.

"Thanks," he mutters, shifting slightly. Then he smirks, but there's something real underneath it. "You are, too. You're, like smarter than all of us combined."

Ava smiles, and for the first time that night, it reaches her eyes, warming something inside her that's been cold for too long.

"Don't tell Piper that," she says lightly. "She'll fight me for the title."

Eli chuckles, shaking his head, and the sound makes her chest feel just a little lighter.

Ava leans forward, resting her arms on the cluttered table, the dim glow of her laptop casting soft shadows across her face. The weight of everything still lingers, but there's a steadiness now, something more certain.

"So, what now?" she asks, her voice quieter, more measured.

Eli exhales, dragging a hand through his already messy hair as he thinks. The laptop screen flickers, reflecting in his tired eyes.

"Now?" he repeats, rolling the word over like he's testing its weight. "Now we go all in. Like Piper said. But we do it smart. We protect them."

Ava nods, her fingers tracing absent patterns on the table's surface. "And each other."

Eli looks at her then, really looks—no jokes, no smirks, just something solid, something real.

"Yeah." His voice is steady, sure. "Each other."

A sudden crash outside shatters the quiet— metal clattering against the pavement, sharp and jarring. Perhaps it was just a trash can knocked over in the alley, or maybe the wind had rattled something loose.

However, it causes both of them to freeze.

Ava's head snaps toward Eli, her eyes wide,

pulse spiking in her throat.

"Think it's them?" she whispers, barely breathing the words.

Eli doesn't answer right away. He moves toward the window, carefully, deliberately, peeling back the curtain just enough to look outside.

The alley is empty. The streetlights cast long, shifting shadows against the pavement, stretching between the buildings like something alive. He doesn't see anyone.

But for the first time, the dark feels like it's watching back.

He steps away, his voice low. "We should be careful."

Ava nods, barely audible. "Yeah."

Eli eases back into his seat, and when he does, they exchange a long, weighted look—a silent agreement.

Whatever comes next, they're in it now.

And they're not going to let Piper and Slater stand alone.

Chapter 21

No Turning Back

The next time they all meet, it's in Piper's living room, the curtains drawn tight like a shield against the outside world. The air feels thick, humming with unspoken tension. The old couch sags slightly under Piper and Slater's weight. The coffee table is cluttered with empty soda cans, an open bag of pretzels that no one is really eating, and a tangle of charging cables. The only light comes from Ava's tablet, casting a cool glow over their faces.

No one speaks as Ava swipes across the screen, pulling up a flyer. "Whispering Hills Casino Charity Gala is this Friday. Featuring city leaders, donors, and honored guests."

The elegant script and gold-embossed design give it the appearance of just another high-profile event for the city's elite. But they all know better.

"Everyone will be there," Ava says, her voice steady but low. "Savannah's dad. Lasky. Half the people we suspect of being involved."

Slater sits perched on the armrest beside Piper, silent but rigid, his fingers gripping the fabric as if it were the only thing keeping him grounded. She can feel the tension rolling off him, as if he's holding himself together with sheer willpower.

Eli leans over Ava's shoulder, peering at the screen, his brows furrowing.

"And what? You wanna crash it? Show them we've got dirt on them?" His tone is skeptical, but there's an edge of intrigue beneath it.

Piper straightens, eyes sharp, burning.

"Yeah," she says, the fire in her voice unmistakable. "Exactly that."

Piper glances at each of them, her gaze sharp, determined. The dim glow of Ava's tablet flickers against their faces, casting shifting shadows along the walls. The room is heavy with the weight of what they're planning, but Piper's voice cuts through it, steady and clear.

"Look," she says, gripping the edge of the couch, knuckles white. "They think they've got all the power, right? That no one would ever call them out."

Across from her, Slater observes, his fingers tapping idly against his cane. His expression is unreadable, but his eyes track her movements as if he's trying to read what lies beneath the sharp edges of her words.

"And?" he asks softly.

Piper exhales, straightening her shoulders. "And we change that." The fire in her voice is controlled now, no longer just anger, but something sharper. "We expose them. In public. Where everyone can see it."

Ava frowns, arms crossed, already thinking ahead, already calculating the risks. "That's risky, Piper. They could silence us before we even get a chance to speak."

"But if we get it out in front of the right people, in front of the press, even they won't be able to cover it up fast enough," Piper insists, her pulse pounding.

Eli leans back against the arm of the couch, his arms resting loosely over his knees as he studies her. His usual smirk is absent, replaced with something more serious.

"You really wanna take this nuclear, huh?"

Piper meets his gaze, unflinching.

"It's the only way."

As the others dive into planning, with ideas firing back and forth, voices overlap, a mix of excitement and fear, and the energy in the room shifts. The air hums with urgency, their words spilling over each other as they piece together something reckless, something impossible, something real.

But Slater stays quiet.

Piper glances at him, at first just in passing. But then she really looks.

His face is pale under the dim light, his fingers pressing into his thigh beneath the table, rubbing slow, deliberate circles like he's trying to work through a pain that's worse than he's letting on. His jaw is tight, shoulders stiff, the tension in his body radiating off him in waves.

She leans in, voice low, just for him. "You good?"

"Yeah," he says automatically. Too fast. Too flat. A lie wrapped in muscle memory.

Piper doesn't buy it.

Her heart twists a sharp, familiar ache.

"Slater," she tries again, softer now. "You don't have to—"

"I'm fine." His voice is firmer this time, pushing back, but when she catches his eyes, they flick away too quickly, guilt threading through his expression.

She doesn't push. Not now.

But the worry settles deep in her chest, heavy and sharp, refusing to be ignored.

Ava sits cross-legged on the floor, her tablet balanced on her knee, the glow of the screen casting sharp light across her furrowed brow. She's been quiet for the past few minutes, scanning, checking, double-checking. But then her fingers were still.

Her head snaps up, "Something's weird."

Eli, who's been slouched against the arm of the couch, lazily spinning a pen between his fingers, straightens. "What?"

Ava's gaze flickers between them, her voice tight, controlled. "I've been monitoring the casino's digital security just to see if they were watching for us." She swipes across the screen, pulling up lines of code and activity logs. "And last night someone tried to trace the IP that downloaded those files."

Piper's stomach lurches, "You think they know it was us?"

Ava presses her lips together, glancing at the screen again before looking up. "I don't know. But someone knows someone took something."

The air in the room shifts and thickens. The hum of the laptop, the occasional creak of the house settling, the distant buzz of a streetlamp outside. It all suddenly feels louder. Too loud.

The room is already heavy with tension, the weight of Ava's discovery still pressing down on them. But then her phone buzzes.

Ava picks it up without thinking, glancing at the screen. And freezes.

Her fingers tighten around the device, her expression going eerily still, her breath catching in a way that makes Piper's stomach drop.

"What?" Piper asks, sitting up straighter, her pulse already kicking up.

Ava doesn't answer right away. She just slowly turns her phone around, the glow of the screen reflecting off her wide eyes.

A single message from a blocked number.

"You should stop. You're not as invisible as you think."

The words send a cold shiver down Piper's spine, making her mouth dry.

Eli swears under his breath, pushing himself up from where he's been sitting. "It's them."

Ava sets the phone down carefully, almost too carefully, like it might detonate in her hands. She exhales shakily, the weight of the moment settling over them like a thick fog.

"They're watching us now." Her voice is quiet but certain. "All of us."

The air in the room feels different now—too still, too sharp, as if the walls are closing in as if the shadows outside aren't just shadows anymore.

Piper's gaze flicks to Slater. He's different now. His posture rigid, shoulders squared, exhaustion erased in an instant. That protective edge she's seen before settles over him, his expression sharpening like a blade.

"We can't back off now," he says, his voice steady, controlled. "We've got what they're afraid of."

Piper nods; the fire inside her is still burning hot. But when she turns to Ava, their eyes meet, and there, just beneath the surface, she sees it. Fear.

The same fear curling in her gut, the kind that settles deep in your bones when you realize you've gone too far to turn back. The kind that whispers, 'What if we lose?'

A fear she knows too well.

Eli leans against the arm of the couch, fingers tapping idly against his knee as his gaze sweeps the room. His voice is casual, but there's a weight behind it.

"So, we go to that gala?"

Piper leans forward, elbows braced on her knees, fire sparking in her eyes.

"Yeah." Her voice is firm and confident. "We go."

Ava crosses her arms, skeptical. "And how are we getting in?" Her brow arches. "We don't exactly have VIP tickets."

Piper smirks, leaning back slightly, the kind of smirk that means trouble. "Savannah's throwing the party, right?"

Ava blinks, caught off guard. "Yeah?"

Piper tilts her head, confidence curling at the edge of her words, "Then it's time to get personal." Her grin is sharp. "If anyone can crash her world, it's me."

Silence settles over the room, thick and weighted. The only sounds are the faint hum of the laptop and the distant buzz of a streetlamp outside. No one speaks, no one moves.

Then Slater shifts, leaning forward, his elbows braced on his knees. His gaze sweeps across them, steady and unshaken.

"If we're doing this, we do it right. We go together. All of us."

Piper looks at him, her chest tightening, something unspoken passing between them. He's already given too much and already pushed past his limits. But still, he's here. He's in.

She nods; her voice softer but just as firm. "Together."

Ava and Eli exchange a glance, a silent hesitation, and a silent agreement. Then, one by one, they nod as well.

Together.

Whatever happens next, whatever lines they're about to cross, they're not backing down.

They've drawn their line in the sand...

Chapter 22

Before the Storm Hits

Ava's living room has transformed into something out of a heist movie with papers and maps sprawled across the coffee table, printouts of the casino floor plan overlapping with guest lists and security schematics. A laptop hums softly, its screen flickering with lines of code, while the whiteboard by the door is covered in hastily scrawled notes, arrows connecting names to unseen crimes. Empty coffee cups and energy drink cans clutter the space, the scent of stale caffeine hanging in the air.

Piper sits on the edge of the couch, her leg bouncing, her fingers twitching against her knee as if she's trying to keep from exploding. Her eyes scan the mess in front of her, but her mind is already ahead, at the gala, at Savannah, at what will happen if this goes wrong.

"We're really doing this," she mutters under her breath, half to herself.

From his place by the window, Slater observes her, one hand resting on his cane, his body tense but his voice calm. "Yeah. We are."

On the floor, Ava sits cross-legged, her fingers flying across the keyboard. The glow of the screen reflects in her narrow eyes, the clicking of the keys the only sound in the room for a moment.

"I'm in the event's backend system now," she announces. "If we need fake names for RSVPs, I can get them in. But someone needs to get us on the list for real so we don't flag security."

Silence. Then, all eyes shift to Piper.

She sighs, pushing herself up from the couch, yanking her hoodie tighter around her, "Yeah, yeah," she mutters. "I'll handle Savannah."

The following day, Piper finds Savannah at her locker, surrounded by her usual pack of designer-clad clones. They laugh too loudly at something meaningless, the scent of expensive perfume clinging to the air like a warning sign saying you don't belong here.

Savannah looks up just as Piper approaches, her icy blue eyes narrowing into sharp slits.

"Wow. What do you want, psycho?" she sneers, flipping her perfect blonde hair over her shoulder in that practiced, effortless way.

Piper keeps her expression blank, cool. She can't afford to flinch.

"Just wanted to say congrats on the big party," she says, leaning casually against the locker next to her. "Heard it's supposed to be huge."

Savannah rolls her eyes, the movement exaggerated, dripping with condescension. "What would you know about that? You're not exactly on the guest list, Quesenberry."

Piper smirks, tilting her head. "Yeah, well, maybe you should think about changing that. Could be interesting to have me there."

Savannah's perfectly arched brow lifts, but for the briefest moment, there's a flicker of something else in her eyes. Something uncertain.

"What's that supposed to mean?"

Piper leans in, dropping her voice just enough that only Savannah can hear. "Just saying I know things. Things your daddy probably wouldn't want getting out. You think I don't see what goes on at that hotel? You think people don't talk?"

For a split second, Savannah goes pale. The color drains just enough that Piper knows she hit a nerve. But then, just as quickly, she masks it with a scoff, lips curling.

"You're insane."

Piper shrugs all easy confidence. "Maybe. But I'd still look real good walking into that party. And if I'm there, maybe I stay quiet. Maybe I don't."

Savannah's jaw tightens. She stares Piper down, weighing her options, her nails tapping against the metal locker in clipped, irritated beats.

Finally, she exhales sharply. "Fine," she snaps. "You wanna embarrass yourself in a dress? Whatever. I'll add your name."

Piper smiles, all teeth. "See you there."

Eli barely looks up from his laptop when Piper

storms back into Ava's living room, but the second she drops onto the couch as if her entire body is still vibrating with tension, he arches a brow.

"She bought it?" he asks, skepticism laced in his voice.

Piper exhales sharply, then smirks. "Hook, line, and designer sinker." She leans her head back against the couch, arms crossed. "She's scared. She'll let me in."

Across the room, Ava, who is still perched at the kitchen table, her fingers tapping anxiously against her tablet, glances up. "All of us?"

Piper hesitates for half a second.

Then nods. "Yeah. I'll make sure of it. If I have to, I'll play it like I'm her plus-one."

Ava exhales, some of the tension in her shoulders loosening, but only just. "Okay. So, once we're in, we stick to the plan: I get into their network to download everything, Eli watches for danger, and Piper—"

"I get in Lasky's face," Piper cuts in flatly, with no hesitation.

Slater, sitting a little too still on the armrest beside her, shifts slightly. "And I've got her back," he adds, his voice steady, certain.

Ava glances at him, brows furrowed. "You sure?"

Slater meets her eyes. "I'm sure." His voice doesn't waver, but Piper notices the small things like the slight tremor in his hands where they rest on his lap, the pale strain beneath his calm.

She doesn't say anything.

But she sees it.

Later, after the others head home and the house quiets, Piper lingers. She watches as Slater gathers his things, slower than usual. His movements are careful and deliberate, as if he's measuring out every ounce of energy he has left.

"You okay?" she asks, lowering herself onto the couch beside him.

"Yeah," he says automatically. But when he pushes himself up, she catches it, the barely there wince, the way his grip tightens around his cane as if it's the only thing keeping him upright.

Piper exhales, something twisting deep in her chest. "You don't have to do this, Slater."

His head snaps up, his eyes sharp, cutting. "Don't."

"Slater—"

"I'm not letting you walk into that place without me," he says, voice rough, like it physically hurts to say the words out loud. Like he hates admitting how bad he feels. "I don't care how much it hurts."

Piper swallows hard. The fire in his eyes burns too hot, too raw, and she sees it—the way he's holding himself together with nothing but sheer will, stubborn and unshakable.

"I need you to be okay," she whispers, her voice barely more than breath.

Slater meets her gaze, something softer flickering behind the pain.

"I will be," he murmurs. "I'll be okay for you."

The next day, Piper takes the back hallway by the gym, a stretch of dim, linoleum-lined space where the walls echo, making it seem as though no one is listening.

She isn't expecting to hear them. She stops cold. Just around the corner, Savannah and Lasky stand too close, their voices sharp, low, edged with something dangerous.

"You said you'd handle her," Savannah hisses, her usual arrogance tinged with fear.

"I will," Lasky growls, his tone like gravel. "But if she keeps pushing, I'm not above making an example."

A beat of silence. Then Savannah's voice, sharper now, "You better, or she'll ruin everything."

Piper's heart slams against her ribs, her pulse a violent drumbeat in her ears. She presses herself back against the wall, breathing shallowly, willing herself to disappear into the shadows as their voices fade down the hall. Only when she's sure they're gone does she dare to move, peeling herself from the wall, her body taut like a live wire.

Her hands are shaking.

Because now she knows this isn't just a game to them anymore. They're planning something. And soon.

She finds Slater waiting by the parking lot, leaning against his cane, the late afternoon light casting long shadows across the pavement. His eyes brighten the second he sees her, but the moment he takes in her expression, the light dims.

"You good?" he asks, straightening slightly, already sensing something off.

"No," she breathes, grabbing his arm and pulling him to one side, away from the thinning crowd of students. Her pulse is still racing, the weight of what she just overheard pressing down on her. "We don't have much time. They're planning something. Something bad."

Slater's jaw tightens, his grip on his cane flexing, "Then we move first."

Piper looks up at him, her fear reflected in his eyes. It settles between them, thick, unspoken.

"You sure you're still in this?" she whispers.

He doesn't hesitate. His fingers find hers, squeezing tight despite the faint tremor in his own.

"I'm with you," he says softly, steady,

unshaken. "All the way."

The afternoon air is thick with the lingering scent of asphalt and cut grass, the distant shouts of students fading behind them as Piper and Slater step off the school grounds. The sun hangs low, stretching their shadows long across the cracked sidewalk, the weight of what's coming pressing down on them with every step.

Piper knows this moment when the quiet before everything unravels. The point where there's no turning back. Their shot to take down Lasky and Savannah's dad or to get swallowed whole.

Fear coils tight in her chest, winding itself into every breath, but when she glances at her side, Slater is there. Walking steadily, his grip firm around his cane, his gaze sharp and unwavering.

And suddenly, despite the storm waiting for them, she's never been more ready.

Chapter 23

The Lion's Den

The neon brilliance of the Whispering Hills Casino carves through the darkness, and its marquee casts a sharp, golden glow that turns the night electric. The building itself looms ahead, all gleaming glass and towering decadence, a beacon of wealth and illusion. The steady pulse of music thrums through the air, mingling with the muffled laughter and clinking of glasses just beyond the entrance.

Piper stands at the threshold, her heart hammering so hard she swears she can hear it over the distant hum of slot machines. She's caught in the mirrored glass doors, her own reflection staring back, dressed in a sleek, midnight-blue gown that shimmers like stardust when she moves. It cinches at her waist before flowing in soft waves to the floor, a dress meant for someone who belongs here.

Someone elegant. Someone who isn't her.

Almost.

Beside her, Slater is the definition of sharp, with his black suit tailored to near perfection, the crisp edges of his white shirt stark against the dark fabric. A deep green pocket square adds the slightest hint of defiance, a whisper of personality amid the formality. But his face, despite its composed expression, betrays a quiet tension, his jaw tight with the effort of standing upright. His cane—a sleek black piece with a silver handle—rests firmly in his grasp, more of a weapon than a crutch.

He glances at her, his steel-blue eyes scanning her face, searching for something unspoken. "You ready?" His voice is low and steady, a tether in the whirlwind of nerves.

Piper exhales and forces her shoulders back. The cool night air does little to settle the heat crawling up her spine. The weight of what they're walking into presses down on her, but there's no turning back.

"I guess we're about to find out."

With that, the massive doors glide open, spilling golden light over them as they step inside.

The air is thick with the scent of expensive perfume and aged whiskey, undercut by a trace of cigarette smoke that lingers despite the polished luxury. Chandeliers drip from the ceiling, casting fractured reflections against the mirrored walls. Gilded railings line a grand staircase leading to the mezzanine, where guests draped in designer gowns and tailored suits sip from crystal glasses, their laughter floating above the hum of a live jazz band.

Waiters in crisp uniforms weave effortlessly through the crowd, trays balanced with champagne flutes that catch the light like liquid gold. At the heart of it all, the Gala unfolds in a whirlwind of decadence—dresses swirling, polished shoes gliding over marble floors, conversations lilting like a practiced symphony of power and pretense.

This is the world they've stepped into.

And they're about to shake it to its core.

As they step through the doors, a wave of warmth and decadence envelops them. The air hums with conversation, punctuated by the delicate clink of crystal glasses and the smooth, sultry notes of a live jazz band drifting from the stage.

Everything is polished to dazzling perfection. Chandeliers hang like frozen fireworks, their cascading light refracting against the gold-trimmed decor. The marble floors gleam beneath the steady shuffle of designer heels and polished dress shoes, while velvet-draped tables overflow with champagne flutes and half-eaten delicacies; their guests laugh too easily, sipping too slowly. It's a carefully orchestrated performance of wealth and elegance.

But beneath the luster, Piper can feel the rot.

It clings to the air, something unsaid but undeniably present, like the aftertaste of something bitter.

Her gaze sweeps the room, tracking the players in this dangerous game. Near the stage, Savannah's dad is in his element, dressed in a tailored charcoal suit that blends seamlessly with the other men in his orbit. He moves with easy confidence, shaking hands with men that Piper recognizes as those whose influence stretches far beyond the casino's doors, their power wrapped in silk ties and polite smiles. Beneath the expensive cologne and effortless charm, she knows what lurks beneath.

Then, in the farthest corner, barely more than a shadow, Lasky stands. Watching. Waiting.

His presence is a whisper of something cold, something calculated. His dark suit blends into the dim lighting, but his eyes, which are sharp and assessing, miss nothing. He doesn't engage in conversation and doesn't sip from the glass in his hand. He's here for the same reason they are.

Beside her, Slater shifts, leaning subtly on his

cane. Though his expression is calm, his fingers tighten around the handle, a barely-there tremor betraying the tension beneath his skin.

"Showtime," he murmurs, his voice quiet but steady.

Piper exhales, shoulders squaring.

Let the game begin.

"Okay," Piper murmurs, her voice barely audible beneath the low hum of conversation and clinking glassware. "Ava should be in the security room by now."

Across the room, chandeliers glitter overhead, and their crystal prisms cast scattered constellations of light over the marble floors. The air is thick with the scent of expensive perfume, aged whiskey, and something heavier beneath it all, like a tension that simmers just beneath the surface, masked by the polite laughter of the elite.

"And Eli's outside, watching for trouble," Slater adds.

Piper glances up at him, noting the slight stiffening of his posture. The sharp cut of his suit doesn't entirely conceal the strain in his shoulders, as evidenced by the way his fingers tighten around his cane. There's a flicker of pain in his jaw, a barely-there clench that betrays the effort of standing tall in a world that was never meant to make space for him. But his eyes, storm-grey under the golden glow of the lights, still burn with that quiet, unyielding fire.

Her voice softens. "Be careful."

A ghost of a smirk tugs at his lips, but it doesn't reach his eyes. "You too."

They split without another word.

Piper glides into the sea of gilded elegance, seamlessly slipping into the current of bodies dressed in silk and velvet. Women in floor-length gowns sip from crystal glasses, their laughter sharp-edged and effortless. Men with cufflinks that cost more than rent shake hands with a kind of power that feels practiced, their smiles all polished, with no sincerity.

Slater lingers at the edge, his stance relaxed but his gaze sharp, scanning the room as planned. Watching her six.

Just as they rehearsed.

The game is in motion.

Down a dimly lit side hallway, Ava moves like a shadow, the deep black of her dress letting her slip through the edges of sight. The hush of the corridor is a stark contrast to the opulent chaos of the Gala just beyond and its murmur of conversation, the delicate chime of champagne glasses, and the occasional burst of laughter that barely masks the deals being brokered under the golden light.

Her heels click softly against polished floors as she approaches an unmarked employee door, fingers brushing against the seam. A quick glance over her shoulder to ensure no one was watching. At least, no one that she can see.

With a steady breath, she pushes inside.

The security room is small and functional, nothing like the glitz and excess of the main floor. Harsh fluorescent lighting buzzes overhead, illuminating a wall of monitors that display different angles of the casino. Slot machines glitter in rhythmic flashes; high-roller tables are circled by men in tailored suits, and women drape themselves over leather-backed chairs like living jewelry. In the grand ballroom, the Gala continues uninterrupted, with those chandeliers casting golden constellations across swirling gowns and the polished marble beneath them.

Ava wastes no time. She slips a flash drive from the slit of her clutch, sliding it into the control system. The moment it connects, a ripple shudders through the feeds—frames flicker, adjust, and reroute.

"I'm in," she whispers, barely breathing as she presses a finger to the mic in her ear.

On the monitors, she sees everything. Every

hallway. Every exit. Every face.

Her fingers fly over the keyboard, queuing up the files they gathered: evidence buried under layers of encryption, now set to upload to every major media outlet the second Piper gives the signal. One click, and their secrets won't just be whispered in dark corners anymore.

But as she works, she can't stop her hands from shaking. She exhales sharply, flexing her fingers once before pressing forward. No room for hesitation now.

Outside, the night hums with life. The glow of the Whispering Hills Casino spills onto the street, its neon reflections shimmering on the slick pavement. Laughter and the faint trill of music drift from the grand entrance, where guests draped in designer silk and custom-tailored suits step from sleek luxury cars, each arrival more extravagant than the last.

Across the street, Eli leans casually against a car, but his fingers tap a restless rhythm against the tablet in his hands. His screen flickers with live feeds from inside where Ava's work is in motion, cameras shifting as she gains control.

Everything's still on track.

Then, a sleek black car glides up to the side entrance of the casino, its tinted windows swallowing the flashing casino lights. Unlike the others, there's no flourish, no chauffeur waiting to open the door with a rehearsed smile.

Eli stiffens.

Two men step out who are neither valets nor high-rolling guests. They move with precision, their suits crisp but slightly bulkier around the shoulders, where weapons are undoubtedly holstered. Their eyes scan the sidewalk, the entrance, the rooftop, all the while aware, alert, and predatory. These aren't casino security.

Hired muscle. Lasky's men.

A slow, sinking feeling coils in Eli's gut. He presses a hand to his mic, voice low, urgent. "Heads up. Lasky brought backup."

Across the street, the laughter inside the casino swells, the Gala's polished world spinning on, blissfully unaware of the storm about to break.

Back inside the gilded heart of the Whispering Hills Casino, the Gala is in full swing. Laughter swirls like cigarette smoke, curling through the air alongside the clinking of crystal glasses and the low murmur of deals whispered between sips of expensive scotch. The room is a living, breathing spectacle, with its chandeliers casting a golden glow over a sea of satin, sequins, and silk, as high-society wolves cloaked in designer elegance.

At the lavish marble bar, Savannah holds court. She's draped in a slinky silver gown that clings like it was poured onto her, every inch of her sculpted to perfection. Her lips are painted a strategic red, her nails a dagger-like extension of the power she wields in places like this. The people surrounding her are men in monogrammed cufflinks and women in diamonds that catch the light like knives, laughing too loudly at whatever effortless quip she has just delivered.

But the moment Piper steps forward, their chatter becomes static. Her pulse pounds like war drums, but her steps are smooth and steady. Calculated. She stops just short of Savannah, her voice coated in sugar.

"Hey, Savannah."

Savannah turns, that practiced, camera-ready smile flickering for just a second because she hadn't expected this and hadn't expected her.

"What are you doing here?" Savannah hisses, stepping in close, the laughter around them fading into something else entirely.

Piper tilts her head, offering a calm, practiced smile of her own. The kind of smile that says she sees through the glitter and gold.

"Just thought I'd enjoy the party. Big night, huh? All Daddy's friends in one place."

The air between them tightens.

Savannah's emerald eyes flash, her spine stiffening like she's just been shoved off script. "You need to leave. Now."

Piper exhales a soft, almost amused breath. "Oh, but I haven't even said hi to your dad yet." Her head tilts, her voice laced with something dangerously close to mockery. "Bet he'd love to see me."

That does it.

Savannah's fingers clamp around Piper's arm, nails biting through fabric hard enough to bruise. It's hard enough to make a point.

"You think you're tough, Piper?" Savannah hisses, voice razor-thin and venom-laced. "You think you can play in this world? You're nothing."

Piper barely blinks.

Instead, she leans in, the space between them sharpening into a battlefield, her words like ice against Savannah's ear.

"I've got proof. Everything your dad's done. Everything Lasky's done. And when I'm finished here?"** Her breath is cold, deliberate. "Everyone will know."

Savannah's face drains of color, the blood retreating from her perfectly sculpted features.

The game has changed.

And she knows it.

Savannah's breath hitches, her voice dropping to a whisper, barely more than a thread of sound.

"You're bluffing," she breathes, but the words tremble at the edges, cracking just enough to betray the doubt creeping in.

Piper doesn't answer. She just smiles a slow, knowing kind of smile that isn't rushed or uncertain. The kind that says she isn't bluffing at all.

And Savannah knows it.

Across the glittering ballroom, Slater keeps his eyes locked on Piper, his grip tightening around his cane the moment Savannah's nails dig into her arm. If she tries it again, if she so much as breathes wrong, he's ready to move.

Or at least, he should be. But his legs have other plans. A vicious, searing burn tears through his thigh, locking his muscles like iron chains, unrelenting, merciless. It's worse than usual, with a hot, electric pain spreading like wildfire, his body betraying him at the worst possible moment.

His fingers squeeze the cane so hard his knuckles turn white, and his breath becomes sharp and shallow. A fresh wave of nausea rolls through him, a cruel undercurrent beneath the luxury and laughter filling the room.

Not now. Not now.

He swallows hard, forcing himself to stay upright to keep his vision clear. Because Piper is out there, in the lion's den, and if something goes wrong and if she needs him. He must move.

Piper turns on her heel, shaking off the lingering chill of Savannah's words, her pulse steadying as she sets her sights on the stage. The weight of the room presses in, all of it: the gilded chandeliers, the swirling gowns, the air thick with power and pretense. Every step forward feels like peeling back the casino's polished veneer, exposing the decay underneath.

Then, a shadow moves into her path. Lasky. He steps in smoothly, cutting off her escape like a door slamming shut. His suit is sleek, black as night, the fabric barely shifting as he moves. He smiles, all teeth, like a shark, a predator in silk.

"Piper," he greets her, his voice dripping with amusement like he's enjoying a private joke only he understands. "So good to see you again."

A familiar cold nausea twists in her gut, but she doesn't let it show. She meets his gaze with a look of ice and iron, tilting her chin just enough to keep from feeling small.

"Wish I could say the same."

His smile sharpens, a razor's edge disguised as charm. He leans in, the scent of expensive cologne failing to mask the rot underneath. His voice drops, low and smooth, but there's nothing casual about it.

"You don't know what game you're playing, little girl." His breath is warm against her skin, but his words are as cold as frost. "Walk away now, and maybe you don't get hurt."

Her heart hammers against her ribs so loud she's sure he can hear it. But her hands stay steady, her stance unshaken.

She lifts her chin higher, her voice even, unwavering.

"I'm not the one who should be scared."

A moment of silence stretches between them, taut as a pulled wire.

Then Piper smiles, "You are."

In the dim glow of the security room, Ava's pulse thrums in her ears, almost drowning out the quiet hum of the monitors surrounding her. The screens flicker, casting fractured light across her face, showing every angle of the casino, every corridor, every trap waiting to spring.

At the center of it all, Piper and Lasky are locked in a standoff, frozen in the gilded chaos of the Gala.

Ava's finger hovers over the key, her breath shallow. One press and everything they've gathered—the files, the transactions, the hidden truths wrapped in silk and blood will flood every media outlet, every social platform, and every police tip line in the city.

The weight of it sits heavy on her chest.

"Piper, say the word," Ava whispers, barely breathing, the words barely more than static in the comms.

Then Eli's voice crackles through their earpieces, sharp and urgent, "Guys, those men are moving in. Fast."

Ava's stomach twists. On the monitors, she sees them: Lasky's muscle, pushing through the sea of glittering gowns and polished suits, their movements too controlled, too precise.

Piper stands her ground, her hands trembling at her sides, but her eyes burn with fire.

She meets Lasky's gaze, her pulse a war drum in her ears. And then—she makes the choice. Her voice is clear. Steady. Unshaken, "Do it."

Ava presses the button.

And the world begins to burn.

Chapter 24

In the Seconds Before
Everything Falls

PIPER

The air is thick with the kind of hush that only exists right before everything shatters. A fragile, electric silence, coiled and waiting.

Piper stands in the heart of the casino ballroom, where chandeliers scatter golden light across polished floors. The murmur of conversation swells and dips like an uneasy tide. Glasses clink. The slow croon of a jazz singer drapes over the room like silk.

But beneath it all, her ears are ringing.

Lasky smiles at her, but it's not a genuine smile but a blade, curling at the edges, already slicing through the moment. He knows. He knows something is coming, that the ground beneath them is about to break open, and still, he believes he's already won.

Her heartbeat slams against her ribs so hard she swears it's visible through the fabric of her dress. But she won't let him see. She won't let him know.

She thinks of that girl, the one they dragged out behind the hotel, limbs limp, swallowed by darkness. The one she couldn't save.

Not again. Not this time.

And Slater, somewhere behind her, gripping his cane as if it were the only thing holding him upright. The thought makes her stomach lurch. She's not afraid for herself. She's worried for him.

Because if this goes wrong, if everything ignites the way she knows it will, he won't get out of here fast enough. And she's not leaving him behind.

Her fingers twitch at her sides, restless, itching for action. Across the room, by the bar, Savannah's wide, pale eyes lock onto hers, horror stretching across her delicate face. She already knows. She already sees the fire catching.

Good.

Piper draws in a slow breath, straightens her spine like a steel beam, and meets Lasky's gaze head-on. Unflinching. Unshaken.

"You should be scared," she whispers.

Because inside, where no one can see—

She is a hurricane, barely contained.

SLATER

From across the room, Slater sees Piper standing before Lasky, her spine straight as a blade, chin tipped just enough to look untouchable. Unshakable. But he knows better.

He knows she's holding herself together with nothing but raw nerves and sheer, reckless defiance. He knows the fire in her eyes is just a mask for the storm raging beneath.

And he's never wanted to cross a room so badly in his life. But his leg is on fire. The nerves misfire, his muscles lock, and every step feels like dragging himself through quicksand. He presses harder on his cane, jaw clenched so tight it aches. Every instinct in him screams to move, to be at her side before this whole thing goes up in flames.

She shouldn't have to do this alone.

He promised she wouldn't.

"You're not alone anymore, remember?"

His grip tightens on the cane until his knuckles burn, but he keeps his eyes on her, unwavering. Because if she falls, he'll be there. Even if it kills him. Even if he must crawl.

His heartbeat pounds like a war drum, each

thud syncing with the heat in his chest.

He's scared. More scared than he'll ever admit.

Not of Lasky. Of losing her. Of something happening to her because he wasn't fast enough.

He watches as she squares her shoulders, staring Lasky down like he's already lost. His chest swells with something tangled like pride, fear, helplessness.

She's so brave. She's so reckless. And she's his.

Not in the way someone owns another person, but in the way, that means if anyone dares to touch her, they'll have to go through him first.

Even if it breaks him.

PIPER

She glanced over her shoulder for half a second, just enough to see Slater watching her with that steady, fierce look that's become her anchor.

Their eyes meet. And in that flash of a second, she sees everything she needs to know:

He's scared, too. But he's with her. All the way.

She takes a deep breath, steadying her racing heart.

The weight of the flash drive Ava is working from feels like a live wire in her pocket, ready to burn through the whole room.

This is it. Everything they've been fighting for—everything they've been bleeding for—comes down to this moment.

SLATER

He sees her glance back at him, her eyes sharp as shattered glass, burning with a fierce and unstoppable intensity. The kind of look that says she's about to strike the match and let everything go up in flames.

And even if he can't run, even if his body betrays him, his heart won't.

She won't face this alone. Not while he's breathing.

Somewhere in the casino's glittering chaos, Ava waits, steady and still, fingers poised over her earpiece, ready for Piper's signal.

Outside, Eli watches from the shadows, already tracking Lasky's men as they shift too close, their movements like circling sharks.

Piper holds Lasky's gaze steady despite the wild rhythm of her heartbeat slamming against her ribs. Her fingers curl into fists at her sides, the tension crackling in the air like static before a storm.

She exhales just enough to steady herself.

"Do it," she breathes, barely more than a whisper. The mic hidden in her collar catches every syllable.

Slater sees her lips move. He doesn't hear the words, but he doesn't have to.

Because the moment they leave her mouth, the world starts to fall apart.

Chapter 25

When It All Burns

Piper's eyes lock onto Lasky, her voice cutting through the charged air, low but razor-sharp.

"Do it."

Across the casino, hidden deep in the security room, Ava's breath is shallow, her pulse a hammer against her ribs. Her finger hovers over the keyboard for half a second before she slams it down.

"Send."

And then the entire system detonates. The chandeliers overhead flicker as every screen in the casino glitches and then bursts to life in unison. The hum of the slot machines stutters, replaced by a flood of images of missing girls, financial records, transaction logs, and names tying Lasky, Savannah's father, to the darkest corners of the city. The truth bleeds across every screen.

Above the bar, the massive displays ignite with photos of Lasky's face, Savannah's father's name, and a scrolling list of victims: red-stamped reports, wire transfers, and girls who were never found.

For a single breath, the room is silent.

A hush, suspended, as if the entire casino is sucking in one last breath before the fall.

Then. Chaos. Glasses shatter against marble floors as people stumble back, gasps slicing through the stunned quiet. A woman screams. Phones rise into the air, cameras flashing as people scramble to record. A man near the blackjack table curses, knocking over his chair in his hurry to step away. Some guests stare in mute horror. Others start demanding answers.

At the center of it all, Savannah's father goes rigid, his face turning the color of bleached bone. He whips toward Lasky, whose careful mask finally cracks. His fingers twitched at his sides, and his lips pulled into a look that was somewhere between fury and disbelief.

Piper doesn't move. She barely breathes. Her chest rises and falls with the force of her pulse, adrenaline screaming through her veins.

She watches as the empire they built, the one they thought was untouchable, begins to burn.

Lasky spins toward her, his eyes blazing, his carefully constructed mask finally slipping into something raw and vicious.

"You little—"

His hand lunges for her arm so quickly, cruelly, the kind of movement practiced on people who never had the strength to resist. His fingers curl, aiming to clamp down, to bruise, to remind her exactly who he thinks holds the power here.

But before Piper can even flinch, Slater steps in. He moves despite the fire in his leg. Despite the way, his muscles seize and scream with every step. Despite knowing this could break him.

He doesn't care. With a sharp crack, his cane slams into Lasky's chest, shoving him back a step. The impact is solid, enough to force the man off balance, enough to say, 'Don't you dare.'

Lasky stumbles, his expression flickering from rage to disbelief.

"Don't touch her," Slater growls, his breath ragged but unwavering.

Piper's eyes go wide—because she knows what that cost him. She Knows every movement is a battle. And yet, here he stands.

Lasky straightens, smoothing his jacket, his sneer curling at the edges.

"You think you can protect her, kid?"

Slater doesn't blink. His jaw tightens, his grip firm around the cane like a weapon he refuses to drop.

"Watch me."

Savannah is unraveling. She stands frozen, her face pale, her fingers twitching as gasps ripple through the crowd. Whispers catch like wildfire, spreading fast, scorching.

"Is that her dad?"

"She knew."

"Was she helping him?"

The words hit like knives: sharp, merciless. Savannah fumbles for her phone, her hands shaking too hard to grip it properly. She tries to say something, to spin an excuse, to plead, but no one is listening. No one believes her. Then, her wide, panicked eyes snap up and find Piper's.

And in that instant, Piper sees it. Not anger. Not arrogance. Fear. Real, gut-wrenching, everything-is-crashing fear.

Savannah swallows, voice barely a whisper, brittle and broken. "What did you do?"

Piper doesn't flinch. Her stare is sharp as shattered glass. Unapologetic. Unrelenting.

"I told the truth."

The tension snaps.

Two of Lasky's men shove through the

panicked crowd, their movements sharp and deliberate. Their focus is locked on Piper. Slater.

Piper barely has time to breathe.

"Slater—" she gasps, grabbing his arm, the weight of everything crashing in.

One of the men reaches for her. A hand that's rough, fast, closing in on them. But then, Eli appears.

He's sudden, a force of motion, slamming into the guy from behind with enough power to knock him off balance. The man stumbles forward, catching himself on the edge of a poker table. Eli doesn't back down. His voice is low, dangerous.

"Touch her, and I swear I'll have every cop in this city here in five minutes."

The man sneers, rolling his shoulders like he's ready to throw a punch. "Or what?"

But before anything more can be said, a siren wails outside. Loud. Close.

Everything shifts.

Ava's voice crackles through their earpieces, sharp, breathless, thrumming with urgency.

"Cops are on the way. I sent everything to them, too. It's too big to ignore now."

The words hit like a shockwave.

Piper exhales, a shaky breath slipping past her lips, but she doesn't let herself relax. Not yet, because this isn't over. Not until the sirens stop. Not until the handcuffs snap shut. Not until they win.

Lasky steps in, too close, his breath hot with barely restrained fury. His voice slithers out, low and venomous.

"You think you've won? You've just made enemies you don't even understand."

Piper doesn't flinch. She meets his gaze, steady and unyielding, fire licking under her skin. The weight of everything she's done, everything she's lost, everything she's about to finish coils inside her like a blade waiting to strike. She tilts her chin up, her voice quiet but laced with steel.

"Good." A pause, sharp as a knife. "Be scared of me."

Behind her, Slater straightens as much as his battered body allows, fighting against the sway in his stance. His breathing is ragged, but he's still standing.

Because Piper isn't facing this alone. Not now. Not ever.

Savannah's father is trying to escape. He moves toward the exit, his shoulders tight, his gaze darting for an opening, but there isn't one.

The cameras are on him now, a wall of flashing lights and ruthless voices. Reporters shove forward;

microphones thrust toward his face like weapons.

"Mr. Lasky, is it true you funded this operation?"

"What do you say to the families of these girls?"

His face is ashen; his mouth opens and closes, but the words won't come. He's cornered, trapped, and for the first time in his life, money won't buy his way out. A bead of sweat slips down his temple. His hands twitch uselessly at his sides. He stammers—half-formed denials, excuses, but they crumble before they even leave his tongue.

A few feet away, Savannah stands frozen, watching her world collapse piece by piece. Her breath is shallow; her fingers are curled at her sides as if she's trying to hold onto something, anything. But there's nothing left. Her eyes, usually so full of defiance, are hollow. Empty. She isn't just watching her father fall. She's watching everything she thought she knew burn to the ground.

The rising wail of police sirens drowns out the chaos, but Piper barely hears it. Because Slater is falling, his legs buckle, and his body gives out completely; she lunges forward just in time to catch him.

"Slater!" she gasps, her arms straining as she holds him upright, guiding him down before he collapses completely.

He's shaking, his breaths ragged, and pain carved deep into every inch of him. But when he looks up at her, there's a faint, tired smile tugging at his lips.

"Told you I wasn't letting them touch you," he rasps, voice rough, frayed at the edges.

Piper's chest tightens, something hot and aching pressing against her ribs. She cups his face, her thumbs ghosting over his skin, her own hands trembling.

"You didn't have to prove anything to me," she whispers, voice barely holding together.

Slater exhales a weak, breathy chuckle, "Did it anyway," he murmurs.

Red and blue lights strobe across the casino walls, flashing against crystal chandeliers and polished marble. The chaos swells as police flood the floor, uniforms cutting through the sea of stunned onlookers. Officers shove Lasky's men against tables, pinning their arms behind their backs and cuffing them one by one.

Across the room, Savannah's father thrashes as they drag him forward, his shouts of protest swallowed by the riot of voices, cameras, and flashing lights. His power is gone, and his name is no longer a shield.

But Piper isn't watching any of it. She's on the

floor beside Slater, her knees pressed against the cool tile, her fingers wrapped tightly around his. His grip is weaker now, his body drained from the fight, but he's still here. Still breathing.

Her heart hammers against her ribs as the weight of it all slams into her. They actually did it.

The world around them is a storm, flashing cameras, shouting voices, and police orders cutting through the chaos. The weight of everything they've set in motion crashes through the casino, sweeping everyone up in its wake.

But here, at this moment, none of it matters. Piper leans her head against Slater's shoulder, their bodies still trembling, exhaustion pulling at every muscle. They're both shaking. Both battered. Both are still standing in the only way that counts.

"We did it," she whispers, the words barely more than breath.

Slater exhales slowly, unsteadily, his body leaning into hers, grounding them both.

"Yeah," he murmurs, voice rough but sure. "We did."

But Piper knows, deep in her bones, this isn't the end. Because when you take down monsters, they don't always stay down. They claw. They regroup. They come back.

But tonight, the monsters lost. And they won..

Chapter 26

The Fall After the Fight

The hotel room Ava booked for them is pristine, too clean, too still, like a world untouched by the chaos they just walked through. The crisp white sheets, the neatly arranged furniture, the soft hum of the air conditioning. It all feels wrong. As if the walls don't know that outside, everything has collapsed.

Piper paces near the window, her arms wrapped tightly around herself. The dress she's still wearing clings to her like second skin, once elegant, now armor—dented, cracked, barely holding together. Her reflection in the glass is pale, her eyes hollow, but she can't bring herself to turn away.

Slater sits on the edge of the bed, his cane abandoned beside him, his leg stretched stiffly in front of him. His hands rest on his thighs, fingers curled like he's still bracing for a fight his body already lost. Every muscle in him trembles, exhaustion, pain, the aftermath of pushing too far but he doesn't complain. He just breathes, slow and measured, trying to keep himself upright.

Neither of them speaks. Not yet. Because words would make it real.

Finally, Piper tears herself away from the window, her voice hoarse, raw, "You scared me."

Slater's head snaps up, surprised by the sharpness in her tone like she's angry, but only because she's terrified.

"Piper—"

"No." She shakes her head, moving toward him fast, dropping to her knees so they're eye-level. The distance between them vanishes in a heartbeat. She needs him to hear this.

"You scared me, Slater. You scared me so bad," Her hands tremble as she grabs his, gripping tight like she's afraid he'll disappear if she lets go.

"I told you I needed you to be okay. I told you."

Slater exhales, his shoulders sagging, his voice quiet, guilt worn. "I know."

He squeezes her hands, looking down, his jaw tight enough to splinter, "I couldn't let them hurt you," he says, voice fraying at the edges. "I couldn't just stand there and watch. Even if it meant…"

Piper's breath catches. "Even if it meant what?" she whispers.

Slater looks up, and for the first time, there's nothing guarded in his eyes. Just something raw, open, aching.

"Even if it meant breaking something in me for good."

Piper exhales sharply, her throat locking up.

"You think I want that?" Her voice shakes, thick with emotion. "You think I want to win this fight if it costs you?"

She leans in, her forehead pressing against his, her breath warm, unsteady. She closes her eyes, breathing him in, grounding herself in him. Holding onto something real, something alive.

"You're not my shield, Slater," she whispers, voice barely there. "You're my—"

She stops, her chest rising and falling with the weight of everything she's never let herself say.

She pulls in a shaky breath, "My person. You're my person."

Slater's breath stutters, his fingers flexing in hers before he lifts a hand, cupping her cheek. He brushes away a tear she hadn't even realized had fallen.

"You're mine too," he whispers.

They stay like that for a long time, pressed

close in the quiet, the only sound the uneven rhythm of their breaths still shaky, still unsteady, but together. The weight of the night lingers between them, heavy and unspoken.

Finally, Piper exhales, her voice so soft it barely exists, "I was so scared," she admits. "Not of them. Of losing you."

Slater's fingers tighten around hers, his breath hitching, "You almost did," he murmurs, something thick in his throat. "I almost—" He swallows hard, shaking his head like he can force the thought away. "If you hadn't caught me..."

Piper's grip on his hand tightens, "Don't say that," she whispers, fierce and desperate all at once. "You didn't leave. You're here. You're here."

Like if she says it enough times, it'll make it impossible for him to ever be anywhere else.

When she finally pulls back just enough to see him, their faces are so close their breaths tangle in the space between them.

Her eyes search his, desperate and unrelenting, as if trying to memorize him, every line, every bruise, every flicker of something real beneath the exhaustion.

"I can't do this without you," she whispers, her voice rough, cracking under the weight of it all.

Slater doesn't hesitate.

"You won't have to," he says, steady, certain. "I'm not going anywhere."

Her lip quivers, her fingers tightening around his like she's holding onto more than just his hand.

"Promise?"

He exhales softly, leaning in until his forehead rests against hers again, grounding them both.

"Promise."

For so long, Piper's felt like she had to be the sharpest person in the room always cutting before anyone could cut her.

For so long, Slater's felt like he had to hold it all together even when his body couldn't.

But now, here, together, they can fall apart safely.

Her hands slide up to cup his face, her thumb brushing gently across his cheekbone, "You saved me," she whispers.

He smiles faintly. "We saved each other."

She climbs up beside him on the bed, careful and gentle, curling close as he wraps an arm around her, pulling her in like he's afraid to let go.

Their bodies fit together easily like they were always meant to be here in this broken, quiet space they carved out from chaos.

And for once, neither of them speaks because holding on is enough. Because they're still here.

Because they have each other, and maybe that's the only thing in the world that's real right now.

As Piper closes her eyes and rests her head against his shoulder, she lets herself breathe.

For the first time in what feels like forever, she lets herself believe that maybe, just maybe, they can make it to whatever comes next.

And Slater holds her tighter, thinking the same thing.

Piper wakes to the sound of her phone buzzing nonstop on the nightstand, the morning sun slicing through the hotel curtains.

Slater is still asleep beside her, his arm draped around her as if even in sleep, he's holding her close, refusing to let her go.

She reaches for her phone with a sigh, squinting at the flood of messages, news alerts, and missed calls. Then she sees it:

> BREAKING NEWS: Human trafficking ring exposed at Whispering Hills Casino. Police arrest the casino hotel manager and local businessman Carter Emerson. Missing girls connected to casino operations found safe in the raid

Her throat tightens as she scrolls photo after photo of the girls she never thought anyone would find. Alive. Safe. Because they did this. Because they fought like hell when everyone else looked the other way.

The hotel room is bathed in the soft glow of early morning sunlight, slipping through the heavy curtains and painting golden streaks across the rumpled sheets. The distant hum of the city filters through the window, where cars pass, life moving on, oblivious to the war they fought the night before.

Beside her, Slater stirs, a quiet groan slipping past his lips as he shifts, his body stiff with exhaustion and pain.

Piper watches him, the rise and fall of his breath, the faint crease between his brows as he wakes, "Morning," she murmurs, reaching out to brush a few strands of hair from his forehead, her touch featherlight.

Slater blinks up at her, his gaze slow and heavy-lidded, unfocused for a moment before he finds her.

And then, just like that, his lips curve into a sleepy, lopsided smile.

"Hey."

Her chest tightens because he looks at her like she's something impossible. Like he's still surprised, she's here. Like he's still trying to believe they made it through the night.

"How are you feeling?" she asks, her fingers ghosting over his hand, tracing the bruises on his knuckles.

Slater exhales, chuckling weakly. "Like I got hit by a truck." His voice is rough with sleep, but there's warmth in it. "But also kinda good."

Piper lifts a brow, skeptical. "Good?"

His smile softens, something real flickering behind it.

"Yeah." He squeezes her hand, his touch lingering. "Because we made it. You made it."

Piper exhales a shaky breath, sinking onto the edge of the bed beside him. The mattress dips under her weight, but she barely feels her whole body is still running on the adrenaline of what they've done.

"It's everywhere, Slater," she whispers, holding up her phone. The glow of the screen casts sharp light against her face, illuminating the headlines that are spreading like wildfire:

Human trafficking ring busted at luxury casino

High-profile figures implicated in dark underground network

Missing girls truth comes to light

Slater leans in, his shoulder brushing against hers as his eyes scan the words. His breath hitches, but his fingers find hers, curling around them in a silent anchor.

"Good," he says, voice firm. Unshaken. "Let them know."

But as the words leave his lips, Piper sees it. That flicker of fear just beneath the surface. Because this wasn't just a fight, it was a reckoning. And now? There's no going back.

A knock at the door makes Piper jump, but it's just Ava and Eli, both looking like they haven't slept either.

"You guys okay?" Ava asks gently, glancing at Slater as if she knows he has pushed himself past every limit.

Slater nods. "Still breathing."

"Good," Eli mutters, but his usual smirk is gone. "Because things are wild out there."

"How bad?" Piper asks.

Ava and Eli exchange a glance.

"Some people are cheering for you guys," Ava says. "Like the media's calling you heroes."

Piper swallows hard, unsure how to feel about that.

"But others?" Eli shrugs. "Not so much. Some people are saying you made it up. That you faked everything."

Piper's jaw clenches. "Seriously?"

Ava nods. "Lasky's people are still out there. And Savannah's family has money. They're trying to spin it."

"So, what do we do now?" Slater asks, his voice calm but sharp.

"Lay low," Ava says. "At least until we know who's still coming for us."

"And when they do?" Piper asks, fire burning under her words.

Eli smirks faintly. "Then we remind them who they're messing with."

Later, when Ava and Eli head out to handle the media fallout and meet with the cops, Piper and Slater are left alone in the quiet.

Piper watches Slater lean his head back against the pillows, exhaustion pulling at every line in his face. She crawls back onto the bed beside him, resting her head on his shoulder. For a long time, they lie there, letting the quiet settle.

"You ever think about what happens next?" Piper whispers finally.

Slater's quiet for a moment. "Sometimes."

Outside, the world might still be on fire, but inside this room, Piper and Slater have found something real. And for the first time, as she closes her eyes and leans into him, she lets herself believe in a future where they're okay, where they're more than just survivors.

The sky is streaked with pink and orange, the last traces of sunlight bleeding into the horizon.

Some people still whisper when they see Piper and Slater in town, half in awe, half in fear as if they don't know whether to call them heroes or something else.

Some of the rescued girls are back home now. Others are still finding their way.

Ava and Eli are working with lawyers and journalists to ensure the case doesn't get buried, fighting to keep the truth alive.

They sit in silence for a while longer, watching as the stars begin to appear one by one. And for the first time in a long time, Piper lets herself believe in tomorrow. Not because everything is fixed. But because they're still here. Because they chose to fight, and they won something that no one could take back. They won each other and a future with hope.

Epilogue

One Year Later

Piper stands at the front of a small community center, staring out at a room filled with people: mostly girls, some of whom she helped save.

Her palms are sweaty, but she holds her head high, fingers brushing the worn bracelet Slater gave her months ago, which is a quiet reminder that she doesn't stand here alone.

"I used to think no one would ever listen to me," she says, her voice steady but real. "That no one would care about people like us. But I was wrong."

She looks out at the girls in the room, faces full of hope and fear and that sharp kind of bravery Piper knows too well.

"We fight. We keep fighting. And we don't stop telling the truth no matter what."

When she finishes, there's a moment of quiet

before a girl near the back stands up to clap, and then another. And another.

Piper steps down from the front, her chest tight but full, a small smile tugging at her lips.

Outside the window, she can see Slater waiting for her on the steps, a book in his lap, his cane beside him. Her safe place.

Slater's sitting on the community center steps, watching the world move around him, watching Piper find her voice and help other people find theirs.

He's still got good days and bad. Some days, his legs fight him more than others. But today? Today is good.

And when Piper steps out, smiling at him as if she's found some kind of light, he smiles back because he knows he helped her get there, just as she helped him.

"Hey," she says, dropping beside him.

"Hey, yourself."

She leans her head on his shoulder.

"You proud of me?" she teases, but there's something vulnerable under the words.

"Always," he says, and she knows he means it.

Ava's in a city a few hours away, working as an advocate for survivors, using all the skills she once used to hack into casino servers to protect now people who can't defend themselves. Ava's still sharp, still fierce, but now she's using it to build, not just tear down.

Eli's still in town, quietly working behind the scenes. He keeps track of the dark corners of the internet, like the places where people like Lasky once hid. And he makes sure no one like that can ever hide again.

For Slater, some nights, he still jokes around, pretending like nothing touches him, but Piper knows better. She knows he's the kind of person who would burn down the world to protect the people he cares about.

Together

Sometimes, on quieter days, the four of them still meet at the diner. They sit in the corner booth, just like they used to, but now the weight in their eyes has lifted a little.

Piper will roll her eyes as Eli makes some dumb jokes. Ava will pretend to scold them but can't hide her smile.

And Slater will sit next to Piper, his hand quietly laced with hers under the table like a secret just for them.

There are still battles to win. But for now, they're here together, and that's enough.

About the Authors

Angela Grey is a Native American novelist, mystery writer, memoirist, and poet who has created memorable, moving tales about the sometimes unexpected and challenging road to first love. She enjoys budget travel, camping, yoga, BBQing/grilling with family, and spirituality classes.

Website: angelagrey.com
Instagram: angelaellengrey
Facebook: angelaellengrey
Twitter: @AngelaEllenGrey
Tiktok: @authorAngelaGrey

Paige Peterson received her bachelor's in psychology from the University of St. Thomas and an additional bachelor's from Rasmussen University. She resides in a Minneapolis suburb with her husband, dog, and two cats. She's a lover of coffee, all things travel-related, and camping alongside Lake Superior.

Tiktok: @authorpaige
Instagram: @authorpaigemn

www.ingramcontent.com/pod-product-compliance
Lightning Source LLC
Chambersburg PA
CBHW041751310726
48978CB00011BB/394